GAZA, WYOMING

A Novel

First Printing, 2015

Cover illustration: Ana Benaroya
Copy-editing and proofreading: Silvija Ozols

ISBN 978-0-692-48474-6

"Most towns are the product of history. ... But these new working-class estates, on the outskirts of towns, are like planets which have fallen suddenly from the sky, with a new discipline and new customs. ... People there are entangled in a network of intrigue and espionage. Oppression stifles them. Municipal employees or spies from the factories come among them, engaged on investigations. Trickery is needed to get accommodations in these tenements, and to remain there."

—Paul Nizan, *Le Cheval de Troie*

GAZA, WYOMING

Seth Colter Walls

CHAPTER ONE:

CAMP ECHO CIVILIAN PARKING LOT,
GAZA, WYOMING
TUESDAY, AUGUST 4, 2015

In the months since the rapid construction of Wyoming's Palestinian internment camps, Persia VanSlyke had often wondered what the non-citizen zones looked like. Given the Romney administration's near-total media blackout during the last year, citizens had relied on imagination when discussing the camps and the fresh ring of domestic prisons that now surrounded the Palestinians. This was all newly built not just in the nation's interior west, but also in the minds of America's voting population. On this level, Persia, the top investigator for the Democratic Senatorial Campaign Committee, was a Regular American. For hir, such commonality was an experience rare enough to consider savoring.

Tonight, though, Persia would be shed of even this limited civic belonging. Ze would get, at minimum, a few dozen views of an encampment inside Gaza, Wyoming. Some citizens, ze knew, pictured internment zones akin to the faux-Arab outdoor hovel-and-marketplace sets (actually housed in California) that had been popular with a variety of post-9/11 scripted-TV producers. Other individuals envisioned the high-security-prison landscapes featured in different cable dramas having nothing to do with the Middle East. The rest of the public did not know what to imagine, though even those without guesses privately wondered whether their children—or they themselves—might want to take advantage of the student-loan debt relief that was being made available to citizens who indentured themselves as support staff inside the internment zone. Turning yourself in to one of these new debtors' prisons wasn't such a bad exchange. You lost the right to vote while you toiled in Gaza, Wyoming. But at least each maxed-out free-market failure could count on food and shelter while working off outstanding balances (for the record, at approximately 2.5 times the rate of a Federal education loan's minimum-repayment schedule).

Persia parked a rented Prius in the exterior lot of Camp Echo, the New Gaza facility that held hir officially approved interview subject. Ze was not inclined to judge hir fellow citizens too harshly for any collective failure to keep up with the past year's breaking news. After all, the Romney administration's final-status Israeli-Palestinian talks had blazed along—efficiently or heedlessly, depending on your chosen news source—following 2014's armed conflict between Israel and Hamas. And the New Gaza camps had materialized upon the horizon of Wyoming's unoccupied expanses almost in tandem with the international negotiations. Even after the average American news junkie had come to accept that there would be an actual, if shrunken, Palestinian state in the West Bank, it took a few days to realize that it could not possibly hold the entire Palestinian diaspora of Lebanon, Syria and Jordan—let alone all Gazans. It took a few days more to realize that these luckless individuals would have to go *somewhere*.

Persia leaned against the Prius for a stretch, enjoying the dusky range of colors stirred by the setting sun as ze waited for the government-contractor escort who would drive hir into the camp's high-security zone. Too soon, an up-armored New Gaza Humvee rolled in, complete with hulking driver.

"You wanna hit the head before we go into Teachers' Row?" he yelled from his chariot, looking hir up and down with a gaze crassly granular in both speed and texture. "We've got boys' and girls'. Whatever your pleasure."

"I'm good," Persia said, vaulting hirself into the passenger seat.

After extensive haggling with Homeland in D.C. and the local bureaucracy in Wyoming, Persia had at last received credentials to enter Camp Echo. Ze was to interview one of the applicants who'd successfully plead for a debt-relief sentence and was now teaching English to Palestinian schoolchildren in the internment camps. A certain Grandin Samuels. Hir boss's nephew. This was an off-the-books operation for the Democratic Senatorial Campaign Committee, Persia knew. Not because it was too dark or sensitive to keep track of officially—but because it had nothing to do with getting Democrats elected to the Senate. Checking in on this 25-year-old was just a favor to the kid's mother.

Really, Persia should have been a couple hundred miles west, in Idaho, assessing whether an ex-Microsoft billionaire in semi-retirement could help the Democrats take back the Senate next fall, whatever the outcome of Romney's reelection bid. Typically, ze'd have objected to a task as unrelated to the general thrust of hir mission as this one—but ze did rather covet the chance to look around the New Gaza digs. The potential senatorial candidate in Idaho could wait an extra night.

Persia's driver checked in at the main security gates and drove on, into the non-citizen zone. The architecture recalled nothing so much as a low-to-the-ground office park. For a second it seemed unduly banal, until Persia recalled how the president had sold this grand construction project to the country as all but prophesied by his experience managing the construction of an Olympic village in Salt Lake City. *Of fucking course*, ze thought. Rewriting this many of the nation's rules was not an exercise in poetry. It was project management.

Looking around the administrative Humvee, ze noticed a glossy 8-by-11 brochure in the passenger-door side pocket and picked it up, the better to avoid further conversation with hir driver. It was an in-house publication, the equivalent of a magazine produced by the media arm of an elite day spa. (As in America proper, Persia thought, the correct play here was to look as high-class as possible, no matter the conceptual disjunction.)

The front cover featured what looked like a Palestinian kindergarten class, happily engaged in full-on arts-and-crafts mode. Included within the document's overall page count was a "letter from the editor"–style opening essay from Warden Hugh Lovegren, the overseer of this particular New Gaza camp. The centerfold of the 40-page, thick-cut issue of *Better Living Through Internment* turned out to be a pull-out calendar: apparently there was a nightly entertainment schedule here in Camp Echo.

Instead of going through the hassle of importing touring entertainers or lower-tier stand-up comics whose names Persia might have recognized, Warden Lovegren's camp depended on the interned Palestinian population to entertain itself. There were

Arabic rock bands and jazz outfits. Classical ensembles on alternating weekday evenings. Marketplaces on Saturday. Assorted activities for the Whole Interned Family dotted the late afternoons. Worship services, along multidenominational lines, were held throughout the week, as appropriate.

Toward the back of the book a confusing roster of camp-administrator contacts was filed under the heading "Resources for U.S. Citizen Prisoner-Staff and Their Families." Every department sounded like every other one, which explained why Persia's boss—an expert bureaucracy-navigator—had encountered such difficulty in even ascertaining which camp was holding his sister's kid.

Despite the hackle-raising material, Persia was not quite able to hate the place at first blush. Surely the camps had created shovel-ready jobs, ones that the economy still needed quite badly. And hardly anyone could deny that a small, West Bank Palestinian state was better than none at all. The American public and commentariat had been demanding Big Ideas from Romney ever since he stepped into the Oval Office. Well, he had given them one, hadn't he?

The Democrats had been dashing about in an uncoordinated fashion for all of 2015. And now it looked as though Romney's 2016 reelection bid would be about keeping the peace—helping Israel see that it had been right to trust this scheme (which had left a fair amount of its West Bank settlements intact). Thus proving that, once again, out-of-the-box American leadership—even better, a collaboration between government, volunteered domestic prison-laborers, private security systems and defense contractors—was the world's indispensable problem-solving mechanism. As with the nation's various other hubristic interventionist schemes, the effort had earned a temporary critical reprieve from the public; for now, people were keeping their doubts to themselves and hoping for the best. It was a bad time to be a Democratic candidate, and an even worse time for someone in Persia's job to be doing anything other than scrounging around for top-tier Senate candidates. And yet here ze was.

Given the driver's initial attempt at cleverness on the subject of hir looks, Persia had guessed that the close of their time together would require forbearance in the face of some additional fumbling. But as soon as they arrived at Persia's destination, Captain Humvee just stared silently as ze shut the door. Not so much as a neutral goodbye grunt passed between them in the moments before the vehicle pulled away. Whatever additional commentary the driver held in reserve would be delivered to another audience, Persia thought—and counted hirself glad of this on a personal level, while remaining slightly afraid for the broader world.

As edifices throughout the neighborhood known as Teachers' Row projected the coiled, corporate quiet that belongs to office-supply companies in the evening hours, Persia was amused to find that the inside of Grandin's building more closely resembled the layout of an undergraduate dorm. Ze understood almost immediately that ze had subconsciously convinced hirself that the camps—and their administration—were more professionally run than they probably were. There ze went, another American buying into the Republicans' spin, ze thought.

Even as a card-carrying Democrat, Persia wanted to believe that the country's leaders had this project figured out, like, all thoroughly and shit. Seeing other up-armored Humvees on patrol, ze had felt a quick wave of relief shooting through the old lizard-brain. The joint had seemed secure, hardly the incubator of psychological and physical abuse that one's darkest fears might have predicted. But then ze went through security at the building's front desk. A metal detector. A wanding by a half-sleepy, overweight male guard—who took no notice of the "N" displayed in the gender field on hir driver's license. It was no more serious than what you might endure at a county courthouse. Lots of room for abuse in a system so lax, ze thought to hirself.

"Enjoy your stay at Camp Echo," the guard said without a trace of irony. He pointed out the overnight guest room, directly across from his station, where Persia would be bunking after hir interview. And then, utterly unaccompanied, ze was on hir way.

Waiting for the elevator, ze took in the anonymous, fluorescent cleanliness of this Universal Dorm. The state of upkeep was only disturbed—or was it perfected?—by a stray torn condom wrapper, peeking out from underneath the cover of a radiator. Persia kicked the wrapper fully under the heating element.

Stepping out onto the fifth floor, though, ze was no longer charmed. The hallway had the sickly sweet-sour odor of empty beer cans stored well past their recycle-by date. And when ze knocked on Grandin Samuels's door, ze was not greeted by a healthy-looking example of young American masculinity—i.e., the kind of kid the Romney administration had plastered across ubiquitous online banner ads. That man-child was a bland, blond chap of solid spirits, secure in the knowledge that here in Gaza, Wyoming, he was working off his federal-student-loan balance at a faster clip than was possible out in the hardscrabble Great Recession economy.

Grandin Samuels, by contrast, looked spent in a way that suggested he hadn't enjoyed any of the spending. The scruff on his face and neck didn't appear devil-may-care, just beaten down. His out-of-date bootcut jeans did not present as stylishly ratty; the wear at the crotch was simply embarrassing. Neither slim nor pudgy, he was the definition of insubstantial. At least he still had a fairly nice head of brown hair (though he could have used a haircut). Not that he seemed particularly upset by this state of affairs, nor in being confronted by a shiny, successful citizen from outside the camp. Grandin didn't even seem alert enough to execute the near-obligatory cisgender double take at Persia's appearance.

"'Sup," Grandin said. "You're from my uncle's shop, yeah?"

Persia nodded. "It's good to meet you."

"Ah, you can save it. You haven't heard any good things about me. Let alone 'so many,' as the saying goes."

So ze'd crashed the full-time pity party this kid was throwing himself. Persia decided not to indulge him any more than might be necessary. Instead, the investigator shrugged hir shoulders. "I do know that Beverly is concerned for your welfare—whatever his past involvement in your life, or lack of same. And of course your mother is concerned, too. Won't stop calling Beverly, trying to get information on your status."

"As you can see," Grandin said, ushering Persia into the center of a rather small one-bedroom apartment that contained a shrunken kitchen as well as a "living room" (really just a pair of beige beanbag chairs heaped under the garish light of twin floor lamps). Serving as a putative border between the two not-very-distinct zones was a flimsy folding table. On the adjacent wall hung a framed poster of President Romney. Did the official government portrait claim that space in the apartment full-time? Or had Grandin hung it special for Persia's visit? A nice little shin-kick at the waning fortunes of the Democrats in the year 2015? Ze decided to let the question pass.

"Can I get you something to drink?" Grandin asked.

"You get to have booze?"

He snorted, without any of the rebel's attractiveness that Persia suspected he saw in himself. "We can't have the internet, phones—or a ballot. But yeah, they sure as hell give us access to downers. Just gotta pass the Breathalyzer on the way into school, is all. I won't pretend like it's a fully stocked bar: we've got Almaza."

"Not familiar?"

"Beirut's finest bodega beer. No clue what the economy of scale is in terms of its provision here. Probably criminal at some base level. Maybe we looted the plant at the same time we scooped up Lebanon's refugee camps. But whatever: it's sure as shit better than Bud. So one just drinks up."

Grandin brought over two opened bottles from the mini-fridge and handed one to Persia before plopping his ass down on a beanbag chair. The chairs, truly, were beat to shit; in no way did they retain even the faint outline of proper furniture. At this point, they were more suited for yoga-ball or lower-lumbar reform exercises (and abuse). But Persia settled atop hir appointed seat anyway, slightly hunching over hir knees, shoulders stretching hir well-tailored A.P.C. blazer.

"Good thing you wore jeans," Grandin said before lipping his bottle. By tipping the Almaza almost directly upside down, Persia noticed, Grandin managed to avoid direct eye contact after his tentative—even halfway respectful—feint in the direction of gender inquiry. Persia knew ze was a lot to take in. (Well, tough!) Though ze'd layered hir thick black hair like a bureaucrat preparing for a proper eventual balding—hir pomaded mane was parted far on the right, and took a swooping path across a prominent forehead before fading down to a finely shaved burr along the left side of hir skull—the 5'6" investigator knew ze did not pass as a cisgender male. (No great loss, that.) New acquaintances, like the Humvee driver, typically needed a second look to check an initial analysis, then expended a third for well-would-ya-lookee-here purposes. Grandin might be a slob, thought Persia—but at least he was outpacing the Humvee driver when it came to handling his curiosity like a proper adult.

Still, the investigator wasn't in a fully sharing mood. "Yeah, just lucky I guess," ze said flatly, in a tone calculated to be free of both prototypically feminine lilt as well as omnidirectional masculinist anger. When Grandin's gaze and bottle returned to earth, Persia saw him shrug, as if to say, "Well, gave it a shot."

Persia decided ze couldn't wait to press him on the Romney picture. The president's grin in his official portrait was dogging hir consciousness. "So you're a Republican? Or is that just meant to taunt me?"

Grandin smiled for a second, before thinking better of it. "Yeah, maybe it's not always up there. Nothing personal, though, understand—at least as far as you're concerned."

"More like you want me to tell your uncle about it. Maybe sting the family?"

"I wish I could say I were above such indirect methods of communication," Grandin said, with a legitimately rueful vocal timbre, Persia thought. He took another swig of beer, and Persia took hir first. Grandin had been right; this beer with Arabic and English labeling was better than its comparably cheap domestic analogue.

"But anyway," he continued, "aren't you s'posed to be crisscrossing the country, looking for Democrats who can pull the party out of the shit?"

"Well, if you must know, I am on my way to points west tomorrow. This is a pit stop. A favor for your uncle. And also..." Persia trailed off as a wave of sympathy for Grandin swelled to the mind's shore. Something about his arrested development—and the perma-undergraduate nature of the surroundings—seemed a grim formalization of what armchair sociologists had spent most of Obama's one term wailing about: the declining labor-market participation of recent college graduates. Twentysomethings who weren't buying cars or houses, for some reason. Failure to grow up. Now the most elite of these losers—the middle-class kids whose parents couldn't find them corporate sinecures but did have the wherewithal to email local congressmen petitioning for one of the limited number of spots in debtors' prison—were here, working off their private-school balances by teaching English to the underage population of New Gaza (the better to assure the U.N. that the Palestinians who had been taken into U.S. custody were being cared for appropriately).

Grandin waved his arms at the rickety desk and pair of bookshelves lining the opposite wall. "You've come to slum for a night, and see how the indebted liberal-arts washouts live, then."

"You must know the whole country talks about these digs nearly nonstop."

Grandin polished off his first beer. "On top of the cell and internet blackout, we don't get a lot of newspapers here, either. Just, like, the broad strokes in weekly briefings from camp brass. Lot of us 'Teach for Un-America' worker bees attended the first few. But...how to put this politely. Attendance has tapered off?"

"'Teach for Un-America.' Clever."

"Thanks, but not my coinage. 'Nother beer?"

"Not sure I'd advise letting camp security hear you bandy that about. And sure..."

Back at the glorified icebox, Grandin smirked. "Oh, most of the guards are chill. The lower-echelon ones we interface with on the daily aren't, like, the tricornered-hat patriot crowd? We're the nonviolent civilian debtor-prisoners, y'know? So the guards are happy to share a laugh, look the other way on reefer distribution. Not that there isn't said to be a trade in more dangerous product. But most of the respective populations here just try to keep the proverbial head down. You know how it is."

"Not really." Persia allowed hirself another 360-degree swivel-head survey of the apartment as Grandin handed hir beer number two. "So, morale is good?" ze said as he settled back down onto his beanbag throne.

Grandin shrugged. "I don't pay rent. I'll be out of here in under six years, debt-free—instead of sweating out a 15-year payment schedule in the free-market wilds." He paused. "I wouldn't say I'm 'happy.' Just fortunate enough not to be suicidal, I guess."

"And the teaching. You into it? Or is it just a gig?"

Grandin set down his beer. "Like, I came in with a mercenary's mind? Here just to execute some credit-rating self-help? But that's the one liberal-arts tenet that hasn't turned out to be bullshit: caring for other people really does turn out to be something of its own reward. Like, there's one kid I have. Funny as hell."

And then he stopped speaking. "You know, you're pretty easy to talk to."

It didn't sound like a compliment, exactly. Persia, who had been curious up until this point, in a general-interest sense, felt hir investigative instincts whirr into a state of alertness. Grandin had executed several attitudinal turns in the past few seconds, pivoting from world-weary to rueful to plausibly excited about this one witty student. And then there was this sudden, total shutdown of affect. As if he'd said too much already. "Anyway, listen to me, I sound like one of the president's advertisements." Grandin picked his beer back up off the floor. "Must not have had my daily recommended dose yet...."

Persia knew it was best not to press him to reveal what he'd already gotten all tight-lipped about. "So, if you could vote next year," ze began—following his lead in talking about the overall political scene instead of the specifics of his work—"would you reelect the president?"

Grandin smiled. "Look, I was educated in basically the same schools as you were, I expect. Even if I didn't come out the meritocracy's other end with an elite job like the one you've got."

21

"I'm just older than you, is all," Persia said. "Had a chance to rise in the ranks, before the bottom fell out."

Grandin put his hands in front of his face in you-can-stop-there formation, as though to underline that he bore Persia's status no explicit form of resentment. "It's all to say: I know the liberal knock against this place. A colonial adventure juiced on steroids of corporate privatization and all that. And, you know, is it humiliating not to vote? Sure, in the sense that I grew up thinking of myself as the kind of person who would never have to think twice about my status as someone whose opinion counted for a lot." He finished his second beer. "But if I'm honest, it's not like the Democrats—no offense—were really going to do anything about my ridiculous student debt, either. And from what I hear, the trash gets taken out more on the regular here than was the case in Lebanon's southern suburbs. So I don't know what to tell you. I'm just a high-school English teacher, y'know?" The resigned 25-year-old let his declaration hang in the air for a second before inviting Persia to finish hir drink and leave him be. "Tell my uncle to say hey to my mom for me, OK?"

Persia had been scheduled to leave for Idaho the following morning. But when ze returned to hir first-floor room, ze could not shake the suspicion that there was something else worth seeing in Camp Echo. If ze was going to kick around an extra day, ze would, of course, need some sort of reason—both for the camp's administrators and for hir boss. Persia was supposed to connect with Beverly over gchat this evening anyway; perhaps ze could soften the ground a bit in delaying the Idaho trip.

22

As ze pulled hir laptop from an overnight roller-case, Persia noticed the camp's in-house propaganda magazine again, stuffed between other vestiges of the day's travels. After plugging hir computer into the room's ethernet connection port—one of the perks of not being a prisoner—Persia re-leafed through the centerfold activity calendar. Right before Camp Echo's IP address showed up on hir laptop's network-diagnostics pane, the investigator spotted an item that steeled hir already-firm resolve: tomorrow was Under-21 Amateur Talent Night.

Because ze was good at hir job, Persia knew that Grandin's witty charge—the one whose very invocation had resulted in his severe case of clamming-up—would be among the participants. And Persia would be in the audience. All ze needed now was to invent some public, and rather unspecific, reason to attend. After all, the ethernet connection in the room had not been provided merely for hir own convenience.

CHAPTER TWO:

CAMP ECHO GRAND BAZAAR,
GAZA, WYOMING
WEDNESDAY, AUGUST 5, 2015

The first personality trait that Philomela Shroud detected in the teenage boy—the one who walked past her without a word and then jumped up on a low stage to begin fiddling with a microphone stand—was the kid's uncomplicated interpretation of his own deservingness. Aside from the kid, Melly at first thought she was the only presence within a hundred yards of the not-totally-sealed-against-the-elements tent. Outside, the staggered, antiphonal sweep of moaning winds was being delivered by the same Wyoming atmosphere that was also depositing dry-dirt kisses on the tent's canvas skin. But the teenage Palestinian took no notice of Melly, did not say hi, and immediately began his mic check as if she were invested enough in his work not to mind such rudeness. As if she'd just start paying attention and help him get his levels right, several hours ahead of the evening's performance, here in a contraption at the edge of what was loosely meant to suggest a Mideast-style bazaar.

Fucking jerk kid, Melly thought.

His attitude may have counted as nothing new in the annals of American-managed adolescence, but then again, Melly was solipsistically inclined too. And with good reason. In the moments just prior, she had been consumed by the precarious and life-threatening nature of her own problems as a New Gaza prisoner of

25

the involuntary variety—and whether or how she might attempt to adjust her consciousness to her reduced civic stature.

The kid's posture, a silent but otherwise clarion honk of entitlement, shocked her out of this rutted track of mind. Any teenage stance, blaring the song of itself in this way, would have drawn Melly's attention (and possibly under-the-breath muttering). But this particular pose was more compelling than most entrants in its genre—especially as it came from a noncitizen stashed away in one of the refugee camps that she was "tending" for way less than minimum wage as a condition of her medium-security incarceration.

Melly realized she had expected the Palestinians in Wyoming to act as a defeated people. Some fit that profile, it was true. But she had formed the hypothesis broadly, on the basis of little evidence, and chided herself for it now. Her mind, in its incarcerated state, was already getting weaker. God, she missed being a journalist. She missed her health, too. Melly was 60 pounds heavier than she had ever been at "liberty"—and was probably 20–30 pounds overweight, in a strict medical sense. If she didn't particularly miss the constant anxiety over maintaining her look-culture status at work and in the sexual marketplace— and she didn't—the problems she used to moan about to her dating-world and industry confidants in New York now seemed irreducibly trivial.

Allowing her attention to be drawn back toward the boy on the stage, Melly wondered if this was one of the first lessons America taught its more assiduous immigrants: how to encourage and curate the positive (or at least benign) attention of others. It was the reverse of what comparatively privileged prisoners like

Melly learned to do on the "inside" to avoid trouble, which was remain unnoticeable. That is, unless one was yet another sort of prisoner: the kind always angling for power. You had to speak up and/or break things (perhaps another prisoner's face) to be taken seriously in that way. Melly had not tried out this mode herself, not yet. She was still nervous enough about the prospect of having her own face broken.

Buh-whump, buh-whump went the tent speakers, as the kid dealt the microphone two quick, successive bumps from his right palm and began the rapid enunciation of what Melly could only assume were Arabic phonemes.

"Just kidding, it's gonna be in English tonight," the skinny but not-unattractive kid said through the mic. He seemed to be addressing Melly, though he wasn't looking at her. Instead, he was scanning the rows of haphazardly stacked folding chairs as though they were a packed house.

At that moment, the jailed journalist realized that she and the teenager were not the only individuals present. Standing in a rear corner of the tent was a slender, short man. Not a prisoner. And, judging by the business-casual look of the rumpled-suit style, not a paper-pushing New Gaza administrator, either. Too slick. Dressed in a form of urban-professional chic. He waved briefly to the kid and then to Melly.

"It's not about to be some 'Don't these Arabic phrases sound funny in English?'–style jokes," the kid continued. "'Whatta country!' None of that, all right?"

Needle on the arrogance-detector definitely being blown off the device, Melly thought. Comics needed confidence, of course. But the adolescent boy's was so steely that it might keep the crowd from warming to him at all. She shrugged; it wasn't as though she was in charge of the night's entertainment. They had simply handed her a walkie-talkie after she got off the bus and pointed to her post on a map: an outdoor "Middle East" "bazaar." (Perhaps the government really had purchased the interlocked tent structure from a Hollywood movie lot, Melly thought. After all, dramas set in the Middle East had started to seem a whole lot less exotic to American moviegoers in the months since the arrival of a new immigrant group from that region.) And if the government ever started selectively picking out encamped Palestinian children to naturalize as citizens, this young man had ego enough to become a fully legit American. That much was clear.

Annoyingly, it turned out that the would-be comic was almost as watchable as he wanted to seem. The sound system connected to his handheld unidirectional mic was truly lacking in anything resembling proper projection in the bass range, and the stage beneath his sneakers rose only a precious few inches from the blacktop ground—but his silence was suffused with enough arrogant confidence to compel "eyeball traction," in the words of one of Melly's ex-bosses, a social-media-analytics type who had been promoted to lead a newsroom and who had repeated the phrase with such frequency that he seemed to be nominating it to the journalism industry at large as a coinage worthy of endurance.

Good for the kid, I guess, Melly thought, remembering her days of desiring nothing more than attention in the raw—from superiors, from lovers, from the all-holy-networked news ecosystem during the incipient age of what they had called (reverently at first, and then derisively) "the new media." And though many things—her attitude toward notoriety included—

were different now, it was true that at one point in her own private narrative, Melly had been quite pleased to be sent away to jail-as-a-concept, if not jail-as-a-reality.

Ever since the beginning of her career, in the early 2000s, Melly had possessed half-hearted notions about quitting the many subtly different iterations of social media in which she and her career had flourished too easily to dismiss outright. Several times a year, for a new self-photographed avatar image that would accompany her self-promotional links to her serious articles about national security, Melly found a new way to twist her strawberry blond hair around her neck as if she hadn't really thought about it. There had certainly been self-hate involved in the utterly mechanistic execution of what editors called the "high-low" manner of a "personal brand" (in plain English, it amounted to "serious, but with a wink").

And there was also a hard-to-renounce pride in knowing exactly how many people enjoyed her act; at the height of her journalistic career a couple years back, Melly had had more than 100,000 followers on Twitter, and her Facebook fan page had accrued enough supplicants that her publication's social-media managers took over curating the messages posted to its front-page wall. Senior editors loved reporters with six-figure social-media-follower counts; such independently successful brands were good for traffic, on each and every article. Managing editors and company lawyers, on the other hand—the cadre that dealt with agents and contract negotiations—distrusted journalists with substantial social-media platforms, and treated them with a suspicion normally reserved for mutineers.

If only the lawyers had been as careful with Melly's exposure on published stories as they had been with the standards for her "personal voice" when announcing her MSNBC appearances on Facebook. The publication's digital micromanaging had been fucking tiring. Initially, after her conviction by a Patriot Act–empowered tribunal, Melly had tried to idealize at least an aspect or two of her future confinement: the social-media unconnectedness, the mental space unclouded by thoughts of her hair (or thoughts about how many putatively serious readers of her reporting might be thinking about her hair). This particular aspect of her predicament had been conceptually fine with Melly—and yet, on its own, insufficient to leaven her mood as she awaited sentencing.

Upon arriving in Wyoming just last week, she had quickly become attuned to more pressing concerns, most serious among them the possibility of rape: a near-constant threat, whether inside the prison barracks (which were staffed by men and women), or when en route to the private-contractor bus she and the other prisoners took daily into the Palestinian areas. Melly's cohort could not claim any cushy, dorm-like arrangements; they were serving hard time. In a development the journalist could not have predicted, she quickly came to understand that federal prisoners here were safest when performing their tasks inside the New Gaza encampments—picking up trash, or acting as crossing guards at an elementary school. The more public the assignment, the better, as far as the non-debtor prisoner class was concerned.

The Romney administration hated her for revealing its Palestinian-peace-and-refugee-absorption scheme ahead of schedule—like all corporate types, the members of the administration were pretty spiritual regarding the sacred inviolability of timetables—and thus placed her in a subsection of the prison that was excessively punitive. On top of that, community intel in the women's wing had it that the mixed-gender service detail at Camp Echo was one of the most dangerous, in terms of sexual assault, in all of New Gaza.

Before her arrival, Melly had not expected the threat to be so pervasive. Her lawyer had made such a point of securing a medium-security internment that Melly had fooled herself into thinking that the standard horrors of prison would not apply in her case (which, for all its seriousness, had the patina of the protected, "professional" class about it). Maybe Melly needed to break someone's face. Or blow something up. That was what the woman who'd come on to her outside the showers had suggested, right? That she could get Melly anything she needed, including explosives. What would Melly need with explosives? Then again, if any don't-fuck-with-me gesture was to appear credible and dangerous, perhaps a fireball of appropriate circumference was in order.

Coming back to the real world, Melly adjusted the right underarm section of her boxy, orange nylon/cotton-mesh work shirt—already sweat-stained early in the afternoon, goddammit—pressed up against her body by the black-suspendered orange pantaloons that likewise marked her as a federal prisoner entrusted with working as a low-level sanitation-and-public-safety officer in the camp. She wasn't trusted enough to hold a weapon, of course. Not that she minded.

31

Holstered in her unflatteringly large left pocket—really more of an asymmetrical approximation of a marsupial pouch, dangling off Melly's hip bone—was a bulky walkie-talkie. Of course, they could have given her something smaller, but the whole idea seemed to be to make the prisoners appear marked and ungainly from a distance. If she needed real muscle, she could radio for a non-incarcerated superior employed by a privatized-security company that drained the budgets drawn up in Washington.

The suspenders, stitched to the pants, seemed stupid—until she learned from a prisoner that detachable belts were not part of the uniform for reasons of security. Still, they hadn't exactly taken the feminine form into consideration. Melly either had to let the pants' suspenders run uncomfortably over her nipples, or else manipulate their vinyl-elastic bands around her breasts—thereby pushing them either together or out in a way that guaranteed more unwelcome attention. There were not, she had noticed in this first week, many female public-safety officers. (What a first-person magazine story that would make! If only she were allowed to pitch articles while inside.) And the few ladies joining Melly in her unusual cohort tended to be older, serving in more secretarial roles inside the schools. Certainly not doing street-level patrol work on the streets of New Gaza, like her.

Melly's brow was sweating more than she'd have strictly preferred. And her bangs weren't looking so good either, she realized (without recourse to a mirror) before deciding to focus on the kid again.

The boy, she observed, had a noble or well-bred look to him. And there was something familiar about his face—though she assumed this was because humans generally like to think that attractive people are familiar to them. In any case, it was obvious that he had been decently well taken care of before getting stranded in a refugee camp. Good teeth, for starters, and then there was the second-to-second alertness that usually only comes if an infant has been shown a lot of attention in its first few months and years. Melly had never covered the Middle East— she'd been scared to embed, even though it was the tail end of the Afghanistan War and she had been told she had the babe qualifications to make the jump to network—but she had absorbed the central-casting Arab look via Hollywood. Especially with kids: Melly knew they were all supposed to have big eyes, gleaming black hair (whether it was kinky or straight), big cheekbones, and some kind of bearing—poverty or no poverty. The shittily reductive American suspense shows of the turn of the century even bothered to make their shadowy are-they-or-aren't-they-terrorist characters attractive.

But this kid didn't quite fit those anonymous casting specs. That nose: so long, and elegantly beveled on the sides, like a British blue blood, and then dramatically bent in the front, in the manner of an old-school Hollywood B-movie tough from the '40s. She'd seen only one other nose like that before. And this kid was... a little built, perhaps? Bigger in the shoulders than she'd first noticed, though dramatically tapered and slender in the waist— and oh God, was she sizing up the attractiveness of a teenager now? Prison makes you do horribly awkward things, she thought by way of giving herself a break, up to and including getting hot for a Palestinian kid who might, but for the odds, have grown up getting sized for double-breasted blazers (gold buttons on navy) from the Brooks Brothers junior section, like diplomats' kids in D.C. private schools do.

That couldn't be, could it?

How out of her mind with heatstroke would she have to be in order to conceive of even a single teenager in this camp belonging by rights to the tony class of "influential Palestinians" in America? All those connected youngsters were probably at prep schools on the East Coast, writing precocious, bloggy op-eds in *The New York Times*, arguing for the naturalization of kids like this one.

Maybe. But then how to explain Melly's fellow audience member, here inside the tent? That dude at the back wasn't here just to soak up the laughs.

Were Melly and that other fellow looking at the comedian or through him?, the kid's silent stage manner seemed to ask. He wasn't going to say anything else into the microphone until he was sure his audience was listening—even if this was just a sound check, which Melly was nominally here to expedite. Melly decided to do her part, at the moment, by focusing on him.

She steadied her gaze on the boy and sucked down the remaining half of her third water bottle so far this morning, the dry Wyoming heat still new to her. He'd better be funny, she thought, this kid who would be attempting something as old-fashioned as a stand-up comedy routine.

"Thing is, back in the day, we made some mistakes: and don't pretend like we didn't," he began, as though addressing a crowd of his own. "When we were over there, and some visiting fucking politicians from France or the United Kingdom or, every once in a while, America would fly over to check up on us? *Yanni,* we might have tried a little less hard, you know?"

There was a space here that was meant to be filled during the real performance, Melly recognized, by a crowd nodding its collective head, and so she shook her own up and down a little now, even though she'd never been to a Palestinian refugee camp in the Middle East.

"We fucked up that play, didn't we? I mean, *en jad*—for real. Putting what we thought was our most Western face forward? The way we tidied everything up, and tried to be classy and shit? Or classy as we thought we could manage. But you know, we should have let them see what we were actually buying in our little shops, don't you? Instead of setting up those corner stores as hastily arranged reading groups for a bunch of our older uncle-dudes investigating the latest issues of newspapers and journals. Like: *Disapproving Beards Quarterly?* Yeah, you know."

Melly heard some slight but real laughter emanating from the mysterious guest at the other corner of the tent.

"I'm talking 'bout we should have showed the Western diplomats all those little fucking cheap-ass things—the Yiddish word is *tchotchkes,* right?—the stuffed animals and teddy bears wearing tight T-shirts with the dumb-ass, supposed-to-be-cute English phrases like 'Touch My Insides,' or 'Be My Heart.' Like, these constipated, inappropriate come-ons that would have been perfect for some 2010-era blog post that aggregated silly mistranslated sentiments between cultures. If only they'd had access to the old-school Palestinian refugee camps: they would have had content for weeks and months. *O-M-G, The Top 5 Cutest Stuffed Animals in Palestinian Refugee Camps.* My favorite one, my cousin had, which I saw once when I probably visited the West Bank for the first time, was a little stuffed dolphin wearing a dress that said, in English, 'I Want to Be You, Baby.'"

Melly laughed herself now, despite not being sure how much this kid annoyed her. He'd been well educated, though—that was clear.

"I mean, instead of 'I want to be your baby.'"

Don't overexplain the bit, Melly thought.

"Anyway, I guess the pro-life crowd in America would have eaten that shit up, if they'd seen it! Not that they still don't want us to be their babies. Their darling foundlings, swaddled in..."

He'd lost his train of thought, perhaps. But the diction was good. The toughness almost appeared lived-in. He was...maybe 18 years old? OK, he was cute, Melly admitted to herself. *Let it go now.*

If he were a little bit older, Melly thought, the kid would be taking a stage-drag from a lit cigarette at this moment. And even though she had no idea how many punch lines there were supposed to be in this riff, she had no trouble at least appearing to pay attention as he continued.

"Which: you know the only reason those things flew in the home was because even moms and dads knew that a teddy bear with an embarrassingly fucked-up English phrase could still be, like, a positive thing, you know? *Bahkti Ingleezeeeee.* Always with the learning English. Why didn't we ever let the politicians see that? Because, for real: it was very charming of us. And since we're not always the most charming brand of motherfucker, we need to milk that shit when it comes easy. Instead of putting it all under wraps and filling our candy shops with serious-looking old dudes drinking terrible instant coffee in an overall portrait that must have just looked fucking grave to, like, 18 generations of Arabic-illiterate diplomats from the West, right?

"If only we'd known how poor and tasteless most of America is! *It would have endeared us to them.* I mean, you've seen all those gritty shows about life on the street in America, right? How full of crap is the average bodega in the hood, in this country, you know? But how could we know that? How many generations of Palestinian brothers assumed that the streets were paved with gold from one end of America to the other? The crazy thing is *our dispossessed asses could have always fit right in.* Starting with American wage stagnation in the late '70s. State Department motherfuckers should have maybe just told us that. Saved everyone some headache. And refugee camp importation costs."

He wasn't as bad as he might have been, Melly decided. He'd distracted her, for a few moments anyway, from her own portfolio of ugly, pressing concerns. And he knew how to situate "wage stagnation" in the context of pre–Last Resort Peace Initiative political history. Not bad. Both Melly and the other dude in the tent—whoever he was—seemed to be into the kid's act.

But now the comic was on to a profanity-strewn bit about the lottery process that had resulted in portions of the non–right-of-return-having Palestinians (that is, 99 percent of them) being spread hither and yon all over the West, including the camps in America, and what it all had to do with the 17th-century experience of Native American tribes here on the same continent. He wasn't wrong about much, but the bit was leaking humor furious-fast. More than half of what he was trying out, Melly knew, was going to be x-ed out by the camp standards board, which was presenting the evening's entertainment. In the context of an appreciative audience, though, some of the material might kill. Melly looked at the tan tarp above, pulled tight over steel rods and almost translucent in the midsummer daylight. There was a good story here, probably. Even though Melly wasn't reporting much to anyone at the moment, she hadn't kicked the habit of dumping her impressions into a notebook at each day's close.

The kid was now confident enough in his momentum that he'd ceased checking in on Melly's eye contact and overall attentiveness. Freed from the tyranny of his self-regard, she returned to the question of how, precisely, she was going to keep herself safe, maybe manage to see a lawyer again, or else possibly, in the distant future, redeem her status, both legal and commercial, in the same grand old America to which the Palestinian teenager also—not so secretly, it seemed—wanted access.

She looked back at the boy, or was it young man? He was no longer trying to be cool. In fact, he was almost spitting his words into the microphone.

"Tell you what: why don't we open the books on the American businessmen who developed downtown Beirut after the Lebanese civil war? They were the fathers of an 'economic revival' that was supposed to make the city into the Paris of the Middle East once again, right? Now that Lebanon's refugee camps have turned up in the American businessman's homeland, perhaps he can help speed up the national adoption process."

The reference to American businessmen—who had indeed played a part, along with the Saudi royal family, in building Beirut in the 1990s—stopped Melly's daydreaming like a single sniper shot drops a moving target. She looked again at that handsome face. That nose. She squinted. It was the same nose she'd seen on the face of an American billionaire she'd once been assigned to profile.

No, this kid couldn't be related to Dennett Meyerbeer.

But it was an interesting thought. And more fun to consider than the probable dangers she felt, at this moment, powerless to protect herself against.

CHAPTER THREE:

BEVERLY STEINDLER TOWNHOUSE,

WASHINGTON, D.C.

THURSDAY, AUGUST 6, 2015, 12:01 A.M. (EASTERN TIME)

For the director of research at a major political party, the midnight hour is not a time for relaxation or moonlit intimacies; instead, fledgling minutes of the fast-approaching day join together to make a shadowy fairground, chiefly visited by the cavorting agons of uncertainty. A director of research is supposed to be the first to know things. Tip off the party. See the potholes and pitfalls before they're under the wheel. And yet each new day brings the chance of a revelation that could throw the party into a ditch.

Beverly Steindler—for more than three decades a loyal Democratic foot soldier—still lived in fear of such failures. Grimly specific possibilities danced across his mind during what should have been dream hours. What was still to be learned about the candidates the party was thinking of planting into the national field of grain? Were there mistresses out on the horizon, ready to swoop down and feast on the intended crops? Financial misdeeds, only halfway covered up? Racism in the background of an otherwise companionable advocate for Democratic ideals?

He had help, thank God. But not enough of it. Even though only a third of the Senate was up for reelection in any electoral cycle, there was always the future to think of—50 states to handicap, at all times. Fund-raising to strategize. Would-be

41

candidates to meet and assess. Not to mention the changing front lines of the nation's politics—which seemed to scramble alliances and make inchoate gibberish out of carefully ordered political agendas every few months. When Beverly began thinking about this series of developments, he often fell into a near-trance, no matter the hour.

The recent changes were not merely due to the overlapping political questions of the Palestinian camps. No, Beverly scoffed to himself. Even *before* the Romney administration had, at the behest of the credit-card industry and private prison corporations, reanimated the idea of incarceration for debtors in New Gaza, there had been a general flaying and tenderizing of the American identity.

This had been proved, in part, by the surprising number of applicants who were willing to enter into New Gaza's debt-relief program. Way too many. It seemed that fully a quarter of the country dearly wanted an opportunity to dispense with the theatrics of making a life in the free-market economy. They would happily trade their expensive romps through the increasingly unaffordable playgrounds of mainstream culture to perform deeply discounted services for the government. Once it got out that such a means of chipping away at one's credit-card and student-loan debts could be executed while living in what amounted to spartan—though largely safe—private-prison housing, all bets were off.

Getting into the more desirable New Gaza debtors' prisons soon became a game of status and planning—rather similar to the late-20th-century process of getting into a respectable college. All of a sudden the government was sending out rejection letters on behalf of its new prisons—turning away the great unwashed surplus of humanities graduates who hoped to serve as teachers in the schools.

The Palestinians had not scrambled everything on the domestic political front as much as they had exposed America's underlying reality to itself. Take the way their presence had inflamed the usual cast of characters in the anti-immigration/ nativist set. (Beverly still chuckled over this, despite the fact that no one at this point was talking seriously about normalizing the refugees' status.) Now certain Democrats were vying for anti-immigration votes—a sorry state of affairs. As for the citizen debtors who helped staff the camps, every Democrat knew how their calculated mass flight from liberty had deprived the party of some of its most reliable voters. Minimum-security private prison was still prison, after all.

For Beverly, and all of his colleagues looking to score senatorial seats, the hunt was on for new methods of coalition-building. Beverly could rattle off inside 10 seconds the names of the employees at the Democratic Senatorial Campaign Committee who were both trustworthy and talented. (In politics, so few of the latter possessed the traits of the former.) But even his favorite operative—the individual Beverly had scouted at a fractious Campus Liberals Coalition meeting at a northeastern college back in the late '90s—could not be expected to help him with this evening's terrors. For the second night in a row, that top operative had also been preoccupied by the New Gaza question. Ze had even successfully petitioned Beverly, as well as Camp Echo brass, to stay for a second night.

43

This was Beverly's own fault. He had sent Persia to the camp in Wyoming to placate his elder sister—a retired schoolteacher in Vermont who had been nursing a grudge against him all year. She thought that because he worked in Washington, Beverly would easily be able to procure information about her son, who had volunteered to work off his debt by teaching in one of the camps. The truth was that New Gaza prison population assignments had become complexly braided with National Security–style red tape, and it was hard to get reliable information about where anyone was actually stationed. As a consequence, it had taken Beverly quite some time to track down his nephew.

And now Persia, having helped Beverly perform his avuncular duty, was chasing a hunch in New Gaza. During their gchat check-in, ze had told hir boss how, earlier that day, ze had recognized the infamous Philomela Shroud working as a prisoner/ staff member in the camp. This piece of information was strong enough to sell Beverly on the idea of having hir root around a bit more. While the utility of the investigation was hard to quantify, Beverly had no trouble imagining the intel's potential upside. *God knows what ze's telling the Camp Echo brass*, he thought.

Meantime, following up on Persia's lead himself, Beverly had found a few other troubling bits of news. He would have liked to have gone over them with Persia—though obviously hir communications would be under surveillance. It had been risky enough for hir to send the intel about Ms. Shroud over gchat. Beverly was certainly not inclined to use the same means to transmit the information he'd gathered since their last discussion.

Now there was no one for Beverly to sound out. He had reached a position sufficiently senior that he no longer needed to

44

go into the office; he worked from home, near Dupont Circle, a tony area hardly touched by the revolutionary change the nation had seen in recent months and years. Working in this manner only increased Beverly's isolation, and gave more power to his physical immobility. He knew he was overweight—he could feel it when stumbling up the stairs to his bedroom, uneasily negotiating the shifting of his bulk from knee to knee, as though each step were his first—but was hardly motivated to do anything about it. He had stopped tending to his gray hair, letting it grow out in matted, unkempt folds of fraying twine. He had few visitors and no companions; his ties with his family were not the strongest one could imagine.

His beloved wife was dead some five years now. His only child, Christine, was busy with her media career in New York. On another night he might have called her just to hear her recount some highly censored and adumbrated story from her brutalizing social world. But as it happened, his daughter had been the one to deliver the second useful tip of the just-finished day—one that, even more than Persia's, was keeping him awake at this hour. He couldn't call Christine, either; she'd be sure to ask what else he'd found out. Her tip, Beverly reflected now, might yet compel him—later on in the day, a day that was already here—to reassign his top investigator.

Perhaps the only approach left was a direct one. The man Beverly thought he could call, in the still of the night, was a man who might have a sleeping disorder rather like that of the director of research for the Democratic Senatorial Campaign Committee.

If he wanted answers quickly—and part of him did want to be convinced that nothing of interest to his shop was transpiring in Wyoming—he could just call Camp Echo directly. Lay a few cards on the table. Would the late hour matter? Beverly expected that the administrator of a New Gaza camp probably experienced nights not entirely unlike his own. Those bureaucrats were struggling to keep pace with recent events just as Beverly was. Surely they too habitually felt the tremors of uncertainty—about their careers, the nature of the Palestinian camps, the citizen debtors under their supervision—at times when sleep should otherwise take over.

The time was now nearly 2 a.m. Beverly had a name and phone number at the ready. It had taken him most of the prior day to lather up this small amount of data from his daughter's single, vague piece of information. He also knew it would be risky to describe even the outlines of his current hunch to a New Gaza boss: that a potential candidate for the U.S. Senate might have a relation in one of the Palestinian encampments. If it was to be done at all, the conversation would have to start out somewhat abstractly. Though, after losing another quarter of an hour to nervous languor, Beverly decided that he would call. The night had proved too awful to navigate alone.

CHAPTER FOUR:

CAMP ECHO WARDEN'S CHAMBERS,
GAZA, WYOMING
THURSDAY, AUGUST 6, 2015, 12:15 A.M. (MOUNTAIN TIME)

Not a single civilization referenced in our history books has ever considered a midnight interruption from a political operative to be a positive omen. Being surprised by a practiced liar with a series of vaguely threatening questions in the small hours can feel instead like the first harbinger of a lengthy curse. It was true even on the best of evenings. And this was not shaping up to be Hugh Lovegren's easiest night as the warden of Camp Echo.

Upon being woken by a call that had come directly to his bedside phone, the warden tried to affect a breezy, nonchalant air with the Democratic Party operative on the other end of the line. Eventually, after exchanging awkward pleasantries, the man with the curiously tremulous timbre—who had identified himself as Beverly Steindler—came to the point.

"Any 'notables' among your refugee pop?" Steindler's first question—voiced as casually as if it were a frequent gesture—was followed by a quick and unconvincing addendum: "Don't worry. This is probably nothing."

Bullshit. Warden Lovegren was aware that another Democratic operative had been one of his civilian guests over the past two days (under some doubtlessly false pretenses). And now this panicky late-night call. They had to be connected.

Overseeing what amounted to two overlapping prisons was no job for those easily spooked by complexities and evasions of truth. And, handily enough, there was a self-administered vaccine (of a sort) that camp administrators could take to prevent the worries inspired by prying politicians and their handlers. To make the treatment feel honest, Warden Lovegren tried his best to be ascetic on matters of partisan politics; he could not even remember the last time he had voted. Perhaps it had been for Obama. Though a great deal had, of course, changed since then. Most important for Warden Lovegren, he had achieved a position that benefited from his affected distance from domestic politics. And so he paid scant attention to the grappling between Republicans and Democrats, but took pride in engaging with matters of *international* concern. This superiority allowed him, when required, to treat D.C. politicos badly, and without a second thought.

He enjoyed this. Lovegren's cultivated sense of remove buttressed his distaste for staying current with every partisan battle, and had the added benefit of leaving him unmoved by their outcome. Whatever the policy makers in Washington had decided or would decide in the years to come, he would be tasked with protecting the basic human dignities of the interned Palestinian refugees—until he wasn't.

As for Steindler's query—it was unwisely voiced, Lovegren decided. Even if the warden knew of an iconic Palestinian living within his area of administration, why would he tell someone feverish enough to call at midnight? In any case, he told Steindler the truth: to his knowledge, none of the so-called Palestinian "notables" were among Camp Echo's population at present.

"You sure?" the man named Beverly responded with an odd, ascending trill in his voice, as though he were asking if Lovegren *really* wanted a lemon pie thrown in his face. Lovegren was imagining a nervous type on the other end, and decided it was best to project confidence.

"Mr. Steindler," he said. "Even though I'm not particularly in the business of providing detailed information to a member of a political party that ritually distorts the nature of these refugee camps, I promise you I would let you know about any notable refugee in my care, were I to know of one."

That silenced the Democrat on the other end of the line, at least for a moment. Lovegren was impressed by the poise he had displayed while remaining uncharitable to the political operative. And then the warden heard, though not through the phone, an atmosphere-shredding sound: a quickly spreading aural phenomenon that called to mind a long-suppressed fart given voice through a baseball stadium's public-address system.

The explosion was surely loud enough to have registered on the other end of the line.

"Mr. Steindler, you'll have to excuse me just now. I'm sure you understand."

Lovegren heard the other man gasp just as he slammed down his bedside handset. Picking it back up immediately, he dialed his most consistently sleep-deprived deputy, Robert ("Rob") Clamp—a recent Rhodes scholar checking off boxes on his way to a presidential run 20 years down the line, probably.

"Robert, first order of business: give that fucking Democrat operative the boot," he said. "A one-way ride to the nearest Best Western. Then come up and brief me on this shit-show. I expect to

49

see you inside half an hour." The warden knew he'd see Clamp in 30 minutes, tops.

While he waited, Lovegren reflected on how he'd come to be back in government service. He'd thought Guantanamo would have been his last assignment. Hadn't seen the Palestinian business coming—not in any shape or form. If Lovegren had been a betting man, he might have placed his money on an Oslo-style resolution at some point. Roughly '67 borders separating Israel and a Palestinian state. He realized now that, even in his brief period of optimism, he hadn't accounted for questions that could have only been raised in final-status talks.

Oh, for a time, the powers-that-be had daydreamed about a lump-sum global-charge-card payment to the long-serving Palestinian refugees' "host" states, as recompense for naturalizing them as citizens that a necessarily contracted Palestine might not have room to admit. But civil war in Syria had crippled these fine thoughts, while only adding to the refugee problem in Lebanon. (And about Lebanon, the less said the better. Suffice it to say that their own civil-war veterans—once rival butchers, now Parliament colleagues—still could not agree on which clans would get the money that would flow from overcharging the public for broadband internet. And so the country still got by with dial-up. The idea that Sunni, Shia and Druze power bases could split the spoils resulting from a permanent resettlement of the Palestinians in a rational-gangster fashion was simply not plausible.)

The swiftness with which America swooped in toward the end of 2014 had impressed Lovegren, even if it did not surprise him. What had shocked him was the abstract genius of the idea behind the reencampment project. Lovegren had seen the efficiency of the national security state in snatch-and-grab operations focused on individuals; he knew it was one of the things the nation excelled in. Likewise, the efficient temporary toppling of a local power structure was something the world had seen American military might accomplish, live on cable news. It was only the resulting occupations that proved to be quagmires. But what if we were just to uproot a population that our government sought some dominion over? Airlifted them into the Wyoming landscape? Into facilities that, if not up to the standards of first-worlders, were a damn sight better than the hovels that had been provided in the Middle East? *Eat that, Amnesty International.* Lovegren had enjoyed the hubris of it all. And then America could claim home-field advantage, for once, when supervising a population. This was the masterstroke.

The normal objections that a forced migration inevitably inspired—that a people were being taken from their homeland by force, without credibly broad democratic assent—did not find mass acceptance in this particular case. The Palestinians who had been barred entry into the new West Bank semi-state had no homeland, nor an elected government. (Not even a diaspora shadow-government-in-waiting had ever had much success.) What could Europe say? Oh, the continent could bitch, Lovegren laughed to himself. But not so secretly, it was glad not to be the refugees' final destination.

Quite quickly there had arisen a new market for a man of Hugh Lovegren's talents. He had not yet felt done with public service (even if his somewhat distasteful recent work in Guantanamo had not been easily forgotten). Spending the first half of his sixties in the nation's private-prison system—running interference between state bureaucracies and corporate executives —had proved financially rewarding, if dull. When it was suggested that an ex–Guantanamo hand with contemporary expertise in managing private-prison labor might participate in this new venture, Lovegren had welcomed the overture with enthusiasm. And he had had the political connections to see the offer made concrete.

He was more than equipped to deal with a lightweight politico like Beverly Steindler. The Democratic operative's opening question had been too narrow in scope. Steindler had only inquired as to whether there was a *Palestinian* of some importance in the population of New Gaza. And the warden had, in the practiced way of a bureaucrat, answered only the question proffered. But Palestinians, of course, made up only slightly more than two thirds of the warden's prison population.

Now standing on his balcony, overlooking the peaceful half of the camp in the moonlight (while a fire crew put out a blaze at his back), the brooding Lovegren recalled a memo in reference to a new nonviolent offender, a U.S. citizen now serving time as a public-safety officer in Camp Echo—and who had just arrived and been pressed into service this very week. She was rather notable indeed: a fallen journalist who had caused some manner of disturbance while on the national-security beat.

By this point, so much about the aggressive civilian-oversight programs conducted by the NSA had been unearthed that average Americans probably felt bludgeoned by the information. But there were still secrets to uncover—even if the number of journalists willing to risk jail for those stories had dwindled. Lovegren made a note to ask Mr. Clamp about how this particular journalist was adjusting to life in Camp Echo.

CHAPTER FIVE:

BEST WESTERN HOTEL LOBBY,
UNINCORPORATED COUNTY, WYOMING
THURSDAY, AUGUST 6, 2015, 1:00 A.M. (MOUNTAIN TIME)

Inspector VanSlyke was not only skilled at hir work, ze enjoyed it. Even if hir job at the DSCC was, more and more, devoted to rifling through the accounts of billionaires—in order to see which among them the party would most be able to help by clearing the field in primary season—it still engaged hir intellect and instincts on a nearly equal basis. And so, even after being on the business end of a hasty and aggressive ejection from Camp Echo, ze managed to derive some thrills from the act of commandeering a rural hotel's fax machine at 1 a.m.

Beverly had been busy, it seemed, during Persia's day-and-change inside the camp. While his latest research document spooled through the hotel's Hewlett-Packard appliance—the ink cartridge giving off a hot, tar-like odor that reminded Persia of final-papers time at college—ze directed a few tentative but flirtatious glances at the front-desk concierge who had shown hir to the fax machine.

This confident behavior was somewhat new to Persia—a product of fully settling into hir genderqueer identity over the past few years. And why not be confident in that achievement? After all, it had taken more than a decade of legal adulthood for Persia to secure this particular form of self-knowledge.

Persia's general understanding of hir situation had come well before the creation of a suitably varied playbook that ze could use in real-world settings. Regarding the nature of being a genderqueer individual who favored a masculine-inflected presentation—one that straightforwardly disputed the gender assigned at hir birth—ze could answer questions all day long: how a certain boyishness had always seemed a covert part of hir childhood personality, running back to kindergarten; how ze hadn't "transitioned" so much as started to own hir more fluid sense of gender; what it was like to live and work as a member of the broader trans community. On these topics ze could essay.

But as someone who was most often attracted to women, Persia had for a period of years not known how to proceed once a desire slipped free from all forms of suppressive excuse-making. What were the odds that a given women would be receptive to hir advances? Was Persia risking a collision with violence by lending voice to a particular hunger? (God forbid you started hitting on an apparently single woman at the bar, only to encounter her basket-case boyfriend returning from the toilet with a trace of coke on his nasal septum.)

The cost of this reality, for Persia, was a temporary loss of confidence in hir instincts. During hir tortured twenties, the act of flirtation appeared to Persia as strange as that old assignment of female gender, engraved by some hospital doctor onto hir birth certificate 38 years ago. An outsider listening to Persia's dating-related laments would, nine times out of ten, ascribe hir slowness to identify potential erotic partners as a descendant trait born of hir genderqueerness, the whole "in-between slash other" thing being a handy tool for others to use in diagnosing Persia's problems, gender-related or not, once ze had admitted to any sort of psyche stress. But Persia knew better. Ze had plenty of trans friends and acquaintances who were sprinters on the racetrack of eroticism, experiencing no problem at all in figuring out which people to fuck, and when.

Thankfully, now that ze was in hir late thirties, the wait time between romantic initiations had contracted quite a bit. Persia still occasionally wondered what life would feel like if ze'd been even more open to romantic entanglement. But this was not how ze operated. Many an existentialist novelist needed hundreds of pages to explain a truth that had always appeared obvious to Persia: that it took a fuck-ton of effort not to go around misrepresenting oneself all over town, on the regular. No fancy philosophizing required. And ze was happy, after a fashion, to spend a fuck-ton of effort getting such things right.

Besides, hir fully idiosyncratic spot outside the male-female binary gave hir some advantages in hir line of work. Almost as a counterweight to the caution ze took in romantic matters, Persia's detective work for the Democratic Party was faster than anyone's. Ze was quick to spot a figure who was not fully comfortable with a self-selected method of presentation. Fraudulent progressives and supposed "fighting for *you*" candidates gave themselves away more or less instantly, before hir eyes. Persia was quick to hypothesize, and hir hunches were almost always spot-on.

With some luck and a lot of effort, ze'd managed to establish a swashbuckling place in the unofficial national ranking of political operatives, hir legend solidified in Democratic circles. In just a few election cycles, ze had become the top counter-opposition researcher in the Democratic Senatorial Campaign

Committee, the in-house detective who was first to sniff out, and then confirm, the scandals that could bring down even the wealthiest and most attractive of self-financed candidates. And if ze found nothing disqualifying in the rich man's past, Persia was the one to promote him to a more rarified office-seeking status. Hir opinion was worth more than any political action committee, because ze had proved a consistent winner. Which is why hir boss, Beverly, gave hir some of the toughest assignments on the docket.

The front-desk concierge had certainly clocked a couple of Persia's flirty glances at this point—and declined to follow up on a single one of them. Extending the enterprise any longer would court a status of undue creepiness, so Persia shut down production on the come-hither-glance line for the evening. But still, ze had to sit there until Beverly's fax session was complete. And Jesus—how many pages was hir boss sending, anyway?

In the end, after it had come through in full, Beverly's research file provided welcome intellectual diversion. Persia had been expecting it to be related to the ex-reporter ze'd spotted at Camp Echo. But instead, the faxed pages concerned Dennett Meyerbeer, potential candidate for U.S. Senate. Persia knew a few facts surrounding the man, but hadn't anticipated his name coming up in connection with the recent developments in Gaza, Wyoming.

As usual, appended to the verifiable facts in the file were Beverly's own scrawled, handwritten notes. Persia flipped to that page first for Beverly's executive summary. *Whispers about illegitimate Meyerbeer son*, Beverly had written. *Could have happened during his Mideast career. But why isn't the son on our*

radar? A Palestinian? (See documents, re: M. Khouri.) In a
Wyoming camp? If true, could complicate Senate run. Have been
calling around—including to the camp that exploded on tonight's
news. Sixth sense is twinkling. Have a look?

A fact pattern such as this was far more deserving of Persia's analytic power than fumbling with questions of Eros at the hotel check-in desk. Ze hadn't even heard the blast before being quite forcefully removed from Camp Echo earlier in the evening. What had felt like a jumble of brusque administrative commands—none addressed directly to hir—eventually resulted in Persia being deposited back at hir rental car. It would be good to put some concrete details in mind now. Ze opened the document and started to read.

Dennett Meyerbeer: net worth at least $5 billion. Investments throughout the Middle East—but instead of being an active player, it seemed he'd become an emeritus figure at some point in the 2000s. Still, his status as a regional business eminence had survived the second Iraq War, the Israel-Hezbollah conflict of 2006, the Syrian civil war, and—last but not least— America's absorption of the foreign Palestinian refugee camps in the wake of the Israel-Gaza conflict of 2014. Beverly's file contained a few photos of Meyerbeer posing with various Gulf-nation officials at ribbon-cutting ceremonies for charitable causes, from as recently as the summer of 2010.

Someone who hadn't survived the region's armed conflicts was Mayssam Khouri, a Palestinian activist and academic whose articles on contemporary Middle Eastern art had appeared in the *London Review of Books*, *Artforum*, and other publications less familiar to Persia. Beverly's file contained the woman's 2014 obituary from Lebanon's *Daily Star*; Khouri had been trapped in Lebanon's Bekaa Valley, where she had been volunteering at a kindergarten (naturally, Persia thought—the woman sounded like a saint). The school had apparently suffered days of sustained shelling by Assad-regime troops during one of their first overt and massive cross-border raids in pursuit of Syrian opposition fighters. Though the name Dennett Meyerbeer never came up in the obituary, there was a strange reference to the deceased's "poised way of entrancing men of all backgrounds, who hailed from all over the globe."

Beverly's scrawled back-page summary indicated that Meyerbeer had been connected to Khouri in some intimate fashion. Persia was skeptical, until ze flipped through Beverly's printed-out copy of a 2005 Vogue.com slide show of photographs taken in New York, at the first-ever meeting of the Clinton Global Initiative. Mostly, these images focused on a predictable crew of cultural and diplomatic A-listers; occasionally, random personages from distant rings of the Clintonian orbit (invariably trapped inside less-glamorous formal wear) made glancing appearances via the margins of a slide otherwise anchored by, say, Sarah Jessica Parker.

Image 12 (out of 15), however, was unique, in that it contained only three individuals, none of them known to the general public. Left to right, they were: Meyerbeer (identified as a top-level Clinton Initiative donor), Khouri (listed as "Professor Mayssam Khouri"), and Khouri's nine-year-old son, "Gus." In the caption, the slide show's editor had described the child as having "dazzled the room in his Brooks Brothers one-button Boys' Tux."

Persia sighed, wishing there had been a way to absorb the photograph without reading its description. But anyway, there it was: a solid piece of evidence to buttress Beverly's suspicions. Props to the boss. Persia reminded hirself to tell him as much on the call ze would be placing after finishing the reading.

Elsewhere in the file, ze learned that Meyerbeer had toyed with a series of newspapers and magazines since downshifting out of the finance world. He was once married (and once divorced) to a woman surprisingly near to him in age (currently 55): Corinne Testington-Marglaze. Remarried already and now based in New York, Testington-Marglaze still edited *Palazzo*—one of the last shelter magazines in town—after having seen it through the worst of the print-publication era's devolution. If Persia knew anything about the world of decor and New York's remaining glossy-magazine elite, the woman probably had a bulletproof public profile—and just as likely cared nothing for politics. As far as ex-wives went, it wasn't a bad sort for an ambitious former international-investment honcho to have.

According to Beverly's file, Dennett had sired one son during his time with Corinne—the sole heir to the Meyerbeer estate, or at least the only progeny on public record. Chilton Meyerbeer was 30 years old and had already notched a PhD in music from Yale. But as far as Persia could see, the man-boy was currently not holding down any type of job. The address in West Hollywood suggested that he wasn't the do-nothing-on-the-cheap sort of postgraduate drifter, either.

Persia almost spit at the fax; ze knew the type. Of course the parents were supporting him. By contrast, Persia missed hir own folks—and didn't know quite what to do about it. Ze had long ago learned, amid the unremitting hustle of hir professional life, that while trust-fund kids as a rule allowed not a single wisp of air to permeate the perma-suction grip that affixed lip to collective parental teat, many of the least affluent (and hardest-working) among the postgraduate set rarely talked with their families. So it was in Persia's own case. Nearly-bounced checks and ill-advised meals weren't the sorts of things one felt like sharing during weekly Skype sessions. Even after hir career had kicked into gear and payments for month-to-month necessities had been placed on some auto-deduct program attached to hir reliably flush bank account, the distance between the generations remained.

More than the limitless lines of credit—Persia had by now earned enough of those on hir own—it was the connection to one's parents that ze found hirself resenting in the case of the presumably indolent young Chilton. There was one press clipping in the Meyerbeer family file related to the son, the sole productive thing he'd achieved so far being a one-night-only, semi-staged production of a chamber opera he had written and mounted at an alternative theater space in downtown L.A. back in 2013. After noting in the lead paragraph that New York magazine titan Corinne Testington-Marglaze had been in attendance, "single-handedly bringing an aura of glamour and 'it-ness' to her son's premiere," a blogger for *LA Weekly* had proceeded to claim that the opera, which went by the risible title *Preexisting Condition*, had proved to be "fearlessly genre-smashing."

While initially intriguing to Persia, that hyphenate descriptor actually turned out to mean that the composition was a stylistic mishmash of "noise-rock-influenced blowouts, atonal orchestral passages, and gospel-choir interludes." In other words, a pig with wings. No wonder it only played a single night, Persia thought. But just before ze turned the page, ze skimmed the *LA Weekly* reporter's summary of the plot. The references to the recent political past made Persia curious—and so, after finishing the *LA Weekly* notice, ze pulled up the opera's page on Wikipedia:

Preexisting Condition (opera)

For the health-insurance term and other uses, see Pre-existing condition (disambiguation).

Preexisting Condition is the first opera by composer Chilton Meyerbeer, who also wrote its libretto. It is described by its creator as a "fantasia on an enduring conservative conspiracy theory," regarding the unsuccessful court challenge to President Barack Obama's Affordable Care Act of 2010. The opera premiered at the Hall for Radical Postures in Los Angeles, California, in August 2013 (so far the opera's only public performance). It was described as "befuddling and unattractive at times, but alive on the whole" by *LA Weekly*.[1]

Persia skipped from this boilerplate Wikipedia lead-in to the "Synopsis" section:

Beginning on the night after oral arguments have concluded in the Supreme Court's 2012 hearing of a challenge to President Obama's Affordable Care Act, the first act of *Preexisting Condition* presents a series of discrete interest groups which, in turn, interrupt Chief Justice John Roberts on his walk home from the high court. There is a "Chorus of the Old and Frightfully Uninformed," as well as a "Trio for Fox News Channel Anchors," the latter of which concludes with an aleatoric[*possible Wiki edit needed: explain jargon?*], John Cage—

inspired[*source?*] blast of music from the orchestra, during which players are instructed, in the pages of Chilton's score, to "make up your own part here as freely as Fox invented its facts during the Obama presidency."[citation needed]

When Chief Justice Roberts returns home, exhausted, he is met by his wife May (a deliberate deviation from the real-life Roberts, whose wife is named Jane). In the following scene, May reveals to the chief justice how, long ago, she gave birth to a child during a prior relationship —and that she has been hiding the child's existence from her husband. She tells the chief justice that the boy, Gus, has suffered from acute learning disabilities and multiple personality disorder since birth. As a result, he has proved uninsurable inside the for-profit American health-care marketplace. May pleads with her husband to abandon his conservative colleagues in their opposition to President Obama's signature health-care initiative, and also to forgive her for the decades-long secret she has kept. The first act concludes with an aria for the chief justice, "Requiem for a Free-Market Believer," which sets the stage for a troubled night of doubts and visions, all of which Meyerbeer places in the second act.

Persia stopped reading at this precise moment and rang Beverly in D.C.

"You have absorbed my file, I presume."

"Jeez, Bev. You know it's customary to ask after state of mind, especially when an operative has been proximate to an explosion in a New Gaza camp, right?"

"Suffering from PTSD, are you?" Beverly said. "You sound alert enough to me."

64

Ze liked the way Beverly never talked down to hir—always assuming that ze could keep pace with him.

"What did you make of the son we know about?" Persia started. "His opera in particular—"

"You want to go right to that?" Beverly replied, sounding a touch wounded.

Persia squinted in self-rebuke. "Ah, right—I mean, yes: that was a helluva find, the *Vogue* slideshow from 2005. Seriously. I wasn't immediately on board with your take, but now I'm digging in. And that's all you." As much as ze treasured their informal banter, Persia did tend to forget how utterly secluded Beverly generally was.

"Thank you, Persia. It really means a lot. And I'm not even embarrassed to have begged for the compliment. To your question about that opera: I didn't think it sounded like something I would want to hear."

"Well, me either," Persia said. "But I read about it some more online just now. And the dramatic conceit of a secret child and a powerful public figure: it can't be coincidence, can it? And changing the chief justice's wife's name to May is odd too. Short for Mayssam, you think?"

"If he wanted to signal something to the world, you might think even a Yale-trained composer of avant-garde operas would try a more direct route."

"But that's just it," Persia said. "He may not know what he intends to signal. He could still be working out his feelings. You know, *artistically*."

"You sound like you want to visit Dennett Meyerbeer's one known son. Is that what you're telling me?"

"With your consent. Besides, I don't think I'm getting back into Camp Echo anytime soon."

Beverly had not left his apartment in a fair number of days, he realized, while thinking on whether to bestow the blessing that his top operative really no longer needed. Beverly trusted Persia in almost all decisions, even if he might have made the opposite call in the field. He respected hir instincts, as well as hir methods.

"If you think it best, Persia, then you should go see Chilton Meyerbeer. But remember that he may not know for certain he has a half brother, as we suspect. Could know nothing about his father's past relationships. If he is unaware, and believes what you have to say, there's no guessing who he'll tell, or if we'll lose a tactical advantage by showing all our presumptive cards to a member of the Meyerbeer family."

"Understood."

"That said: I may have already tipped our hand to one of the New Gaza camp administrators."

"Well, even if so, he's too busy putting out fires right around now. Literally."

"Perhaps, perhaps. But Persia, please remember: one should be wary of dropping in on a composer uninvited. You might be subjected to who knows what kind of noise-in-progress."

"Good note, Bev, thanks."

Ze thought that would be the end of the conversation. But Beverly was hanging on the line. "I suppose I should tell you that my daughter knows we're poking around into this. I don't believe she knows how I'm thinking that it may connect with anything out West. But still. Keep an eye out."

Persia had always liked Beverly's daughter. She was the only anchor on NewsPowMeow that Persia could stand, truth be told. "How is Crissy, anyways?" ze asked.

"Christine, if you don't mind. She's well, I'm given to understand."

"But you still don't watch her broadcast, do you?"

Beverly did not answer. In the silence, Persia brought up the NewsPowMeow URL and entered hir subscriber password, tuning in to the web feed of the outlet's live cable-news programming. There was Crissy, standing all professional-hot on a set, her pilates-produced ass cut off by the words *TERROR BLAST OUTSIDE NEW GAZA CAMP*. The headline contorted and wriggled in an animated zone within the lower-third portion of the screen, which Persia had years ago learned to describe as the "chyron." And on the right half of the screen, an adorable GIF image of a gorilla swung a tennis racket on a loop.

"Wow. Since when does Crissy do breaking news after midnight?" Persia asked the conflicted Beverly—who was both proud of his daughter and no big fan of NewsPowMeow in particular.

"Didn't even know she was on right now."

"Still a CNN bitter-ender?"

"Hell, I don't know. It feels weird to see Christine that way, all made up," Beverly said. "So yeah, CNN, sure. Until they hire my daughter and start dressing her in ways that make me feel uncomfortable. In any event, it was her tip, after all, on the bitter ex-wife score, regarding Meyerbeer."

"Your girl's got reporting chops, whatever else one wants to say about NewsPowMeow."

"I'm doing my best to keep tabs on her. Though I'm told I'm not at all smooth," Beverly said, sitting nearly motionless in his office in much the same pose he'd been holding since the afternoon. "I'm told it's a good thing I have you to do the on-the-ground work."

"Ah, heck, sir. Please trust that I, at least, know you have game."

CHAPTER SIX:

NEWSPOWMEOW STUDIOS,
ENGLEWOOD CLIFFS, NEW JERSEY
THURSDAY, AUGUST 6, 2015, 3:30 A.M. (EASTERN TIME)

Christine Steindler, who went by "Crissy" on screen (and online), was hoping that her father would not call while she was having sex in the company town car in the middle of the night. Beverly had a way of picking the worst of all wrong moments to catch up with his favorite news anchor (whom he never watched, she also knew). And on this night, the odds of interruption were even better than usual, since he had good reason to call; Crissy herself was curious to learn how her tip had played out.

The breaking news out of Wyoming had already screwed up her overnight plans—what with having been called back to the studio after (supposedly) finishing her scheduled late shift and completing her distasteful evening sign-off duties. These were personalized nightly updates for the website-network's top-level premium subscribers—a couple dozen senselessly rich dorks who paid upwards of $50,000 a month to get faux intimate, almost unbearably cheesed-out yet certainly "exclusive" video from her. Crissy uploaded the grainier-than-it-needed-to-be "private footage" (framed from the neck up) to the designated company-intranet folder so the guys over in Community Impact could deposit her good-night wishes to the recipients' NewsPowMeow message boxes. What they did after watching the videos was their business, Crissy told her friends when they, making "eww gross" faces, asked about it.

It was gross, of course, but Crissy owned her decisions, like the big girl in new media she'd been ever since making a sex "tape" (a video, actually) with an ISIS operative for VileNews.com in the summer of 2014. Once reaching a safe distance, she'd uploaded it to the web, and then—moments later—used a satellite phone to call a CIA contact with her coordinates, the better for the national security apparatus to launch a drone strike (which Crissy also filmed and uploaded as a follow-up). *I Took an ISIS Missile in the Ass and Then Got the CIA to Shoot Him a Hot One Back* did so much web traffic, it made Crissy a mainstream-media star; when the ascendant website PowMeow.com started a 24-hour news channel in early 2015—one that featured "adorbs" animal videos playing on inset loop, no matter the report or the hour of the day— Crissy had been an obvious contender for a late-night web-and-cable-broadcast.

It wasn't long, though, before she was contributing across all their shows and platforms (even donning a bikini to present luxury travel segments for the network's morning shows during the northern hemisphere's winter months). And now these good-night videos. At least Crissy's agent had demanded a straight-up 50-50 split with the network, and stipulated that NewsPowMeow had to take care of producing the videos and dealing directly with the "premium" members. It earned her an extra couple hundred grand a month. Meantime, doing it under the aegis of a network brand—even a relative start-up—made it seem less like following in the tradition of the soft-core, webcam-model revenue stream that everyone knew (though would not say) NewsPowMeow was appropriating. Anyone who was anyone respected Crissy for her position on the next wave of news-product brand innovation.

En route to her network-hired personal town car, Crissy took another look at the new contract from Legal regarding interoffice fucking. It was nothing if not detailed. The startlingly muscle-bound journalism grad student—who interned in the satellite room, Crissy understood—had marked it up with vigor earlier this evening, inscribing big, enthusiastic X marks next to a series of affirmative statements that proclaimed, in part:

[X] Approachee is aware that any refusal to enter into sexual congress with NewsPowMeow superior will not lead to deleterious or otherwise discriminatory professional behavior in the newsroom;

[X] Approachee has been made aware of literature available in the Legal Dept.'s offices as to the range of expectations regarding the behavior of senior NewsPowMeow (hereafter, The Company) staffers who initiate sexual practices with subordinates;

[X] Approachee agrees that a request for initiation of sexual relations with a member of The Company's staff is accepted under no force of workplace pressure, and hereby releases The Company's corporate parent from any and all litigation resulting from the initiation of said sexual congress—and furthermore indemnifies The Company against any and all actions going forward, unless the superior can be shown to have violated the rules and regulations set forth by The Company regarding sex between employees of divergent seniority. [For these, see Appendix M: Examples of Inappropriate Solicitations in a Newsroom Environment.]

Crissy opened the door to the car and caught the buff intern picking at a hangnail. He was just a touch too good-looking to be in j-school, she thought, not for the first time. But he'd been a sport to head back to the studio with her for the breaking-news report. As she entered the vehicle, the young man sat on his hands and nodded at Crissy. He was wearing a disintegrating solid-gray hoodie over a button-down red gingham shirt—frankly, he'd done a terrible job at putting together an ensemble. Kind of a blah-handsome face. Thick neck. Whatever, she wouldn't have to look at him forever—who cared if he wasn't iconically handsome, just mail-order-husband attractive? At least the shirt was tight enough that it strained nicely across his pecs. That was something. And he was also sporting so-blue-they-were-black skinny jeans. He kind of looked like an American flag?

Crissy smiled at her driver via his rearview mirror, then hit the button to throw up the partition between them. He wouldn't start driving Crissy and her guest back into the city until she rapped three times on the Plexiglas divider. This way, the new couple would be allowed to find their stride without the distractions of the road passing by. (Sex in a moving vehicle always seemed like a romantic idea, but the inevitable braking and turning often happened at the wrong times.)

"Hello, I'm Christine," she said to the intern.

"Is that formal or informal address? I can't tell," he said. "That is, given how your profesh name is Crissy."

Aw, he was going for cute right off the bat. She'd have to teach him that she didn't want him to be cute.

Five minutes later, the town car had yet to move from Crissy's reserved parking space outside the studio. The purple jacket that went with her favorite yellow on-air skirt was bunched behind her neck, providing her some halfway acceptable cushion against the window, while her hips and legs were arranged lengthwise atop the backseat. The intern was a passably good provider of oral, enough that Crissy could stop looking down from above—the way she tended to do when worrying about a guy making a sudden, terrible move. With her range of vision arced back toward the tinted windows, Crissy found herself wondering exactly how tinted they were. If a passerby stopped and squinted at the glass from a distance of three inches, would its interconnected series of black dots disperse, allowing for a close-up view of the action? Crissy knew the answer was probably not, but the idea played out in her head as in a piece of CGI-animated pornography.

"You should keep going, but I'm going to talk," Crissy began, comfortable and relaxed enough now to unburden herself while he worked. The intern, like a good boy, gave not the slightest hint of bucking gait as Crissy continued, "You wouldn't expect undelivered discourse to be a problem endemic to professional talkers. But trust me: we all have things we never get to say. And it gets to the point that the not-saying of the things you want to say during days filled with time that one is expected and paid to talk— *oh yes, keep doing that movement right there*—requires some creative after-hours outlet for expression.... This arrangement, as you might have guessed, is my solution to the trial that undelivered discourse threatens to become.

"'Discourse,' of course, being one of those words that is axiomatically 'not a word,' according to one's producers, by the way. 'Axiom' in all its permutations, as well. And no shit:

73

'permutation.' God, this is so great...getting this professional language-stress off my chest.

"They really are in my ears all day: my segment producer, her senior producer, and during the commercial breaks the makeup and hair duo buzzing around behind my head, perfecting my coif. It's bad enough I read their terrible intros and questions off the teleprompter, that I wear my hair how they say. When we get caught in a breaking-news situation and they want to get in my ear about my diction. Like, pardon me for having a goddamned vocabulary." She looked down at the intern's back. "Fuck's sake, you know you're not so bad at this....

"Anyway. In my ears all day, saying, 'That's not a word, Crissy.' And it's all I'm able to do to refrain from saying, 'It's fucking Christine, my name.' Why did I stop using it? I thought it would make me seem less threatening? Threatening to viewers at home, like my diction? And the ways I'm bound by work don't even end after I get out of the anchor chair. The driver up front— Larry, he's great, and guaranteed not to be listening in on a muted intercom, wink wink—you'll just see. The way he has to read you the company sex policy again before he leaves us for the night. Like you don't already know you have the opportunity not to come in with me, that it's not part of your job, that the company—ah, hey: too much with the teeth there..."

At this point, Crissy's phone—attached via USB cable to the charging dock underneath the seat—started to vibrate. "POPS" was the moniker on the phone's home screen. Crissy, though frustrated by the timing, still wanted to take this. After gently grabbing the intern by the throat with her free hand, she swung a leg over his head and drew herself upright on her half of the backseat. With an index finger to her pursed lips, she secured his silence while answering her dad's call.

"Pops."

"Bad time?"

"Never better."

"You sound winded. Yet also indoors. I can call some other —"

"Doing upper-body small weights in the car, Dad. Really, it's fine."

"You're that afraid for your figure? It's not healthy, Christine."

Crissy rolled her eyes in the intern's direction, even though she was pretty sure he couldn't hear enough of Beverly's half of the conversation to share properly in her exhaustion over it. The intern was nothing if not a gamer, however, and shrugged sympathetically at Crissy while pulling the hood of his hoodie over his eyes—as if to catch a quick catnap while she attended to family business.

Crissy considered suggesting that he go up and chat with Larry in the front or something, but no, that would seem like she was sending him away—or else reveal to him how much she saw him as the help, which would do who-knows-what to his fuck prowess going forward. God, a man gives you one orgasm and it's like he thinks he's your personal savior.

"You know that's not why I picked up the phone, to hear you whine about how much I exercise and how it makes you fearful about my self-image, Pops."

"Yes, yes," Beverly said slowly. "I promised I would call and let you know how your tip from earlier panned out."

"You mean 'from yesterday,' I think. God, it's late. And anyways, if I'm not coming right out and asking the question directly, it's because this car, at present, does not contain what they would call, in a movie, 'a secure line.'"

"You have your trainer in the car with you?"

"No, just a driver." Crissy winked again at the intern, but he hadn't raised his head from underneath the hoodie or done anything else to suggest he had been paying attention. (Was he asleep for real? Or just being polite? If he was really conked out, he had a strange ability to sleep on command.)

"There's nothing reportable yet, I'd say."

"You would," Crissy spat back. "Fucking party operatives: you're all the same. Take information and never give back."

"I'm not saying there won't be anything to report ever," her father replied. "Your tip—instinct, really—has enough string to it that... Well, it's here I have to make sure we're off the record."

"Fine, Pops."

"I sent an investigator to look into it."

"Persia?" Crissy knew the caste hierarchy of Beverly's aides like she knew the congressional facebook. But Beverly was not quick to reply. "That's some hot shit," Crissy said. "I should expect to hear more, then."

"Before any other reporter, scout's honor," Beverly said.

"Unless you hush it all up and tell this Meyerbeer douche not to run due to the bastard kid possibly coming to light," Crissy said. "There's no story if the guy doesn't get in the ring."

"There have been men weighed down with worse secrets who were elected in full light of their revelation," Beverly said with a yawn. "Say, while we're on the phone—you have any inside scuttlebutt on the Wyoming camp blast?"

That was out of nowhere. What did her dad care about that?

"Scuttlebutt?"

"Oh, you know, rumors, anything you couldn't confirm in time to report on air tonight, that sort of thing."

What a bastard! Her father hadn't placed this call in order to start paying back Crissy for passing on intriguing but not-super-specific drunk talk from Meyerbeer's ex-wife. Not even a little bit. He was trying to squeeze more information out of her, on an entirely different subject.

"Pops, you'd make a terrible detective."

"Why do you say that?"

"When it comes to casual tone, you can't hang. It's a good thing you've got Persia on staff." She looked over at the intern, just to see if she could catch him peeking through mostly shut eyelids. Didn't appear to be the case. "What's your interest in the news out of Wyoming tonight?"

"Hey listen, daughter, what do you know? I've got a fax coming in. We'll chat later. And now I must leave you to your exercise."

"Kisses, Pops," Crissy said.

A fax coming in—sure.

She snapped her fingers at the intern. If he'd been faking sleep, the better to half-eavesdrop, he at least now managed a credible awakening routine: bleary-eyed, and not too much emphasis with outstretched limbs or any of that playacting.

"What say you to this," Crissy began, taking his right hand and placing it under her skirt. "We go to my place, and then my driver spouts some company legalese, has you re-sign the paperwork just before you come inside with me?" The intern kissed her on the cheek while rubbing his hand where she'd placed it. Crissy rapped on the partition. Larry started the car in response.

She asked the intern to go down on her again during the ride home. "I promise you, I'll get you off later," she said. "But I want to talk out loud some more, and it's easier to talk sometimes if I've got a man's face to fuck." The intern took off his shirt— which Crissy liked, except that he had done it before she could order him to. He scrunched down on the backseat, bare-chested.

"I'm sure you'll be interested to learn that I've been thinking about creation recently," she told him as the car began to move. "The idea has become too big a responsibility for most of us to bear. Instead of maintaining a proper respect for the dangers, now we're just full-tilt freaked out by the process of those choices—or of making something the wrong way. Maybe we tell ourselves that it's good to wonder if creation is now totally immoral. But we still want to think we're creative—so now we've become more artful about our caution. We create our own vacuums and call it 'curation.' We're proud about making sure we don't accidentally commit the mistakes we think will spill out if we try to create too assertively."

As she lectured, Crissy was relieved to find that the intern was not responding to her words. It almost didn't matter whether he was just too inarticulate to participate, or if (even better) he had intuited that she was getting off on the solitude of uninterrupted speechifying. This is what Crissy most wanted: the ability to rip out paragraph after paragraph of inner monologue while a man tended to her with his mouth. That was the only exchange that interested her, with this or any other man. Each word she spoke led to nothing else. Each uttered syllable became as immediately blank as every round of ejaculate that had ever been shot into her hormonally regulated body.

"That's the new adult art," she said, patting his head after her first orgasm. "Regret minimization. Leaving open the space for undoing choices. Or else making a permanent space in our lives devoted to uncreation. The most admired friend in your circle is the richest, most accomplished person who has the greatest number of options still open. For women, there's this often unacknowledged respect for the individual who hasn't created herself into some filthy and dependent corner. A woman who is employed and successful, and also has pulled off the trick of family life, might even be this individual—but only if it's clear that she has the strength to leave her husband in an instant, and take the kids, and still keep working, without missing a beat.

"She's the alpha in her social group. She's the one they all pray to be like just before bed. Her girlfriends—even if they have more money, or greater positions—are less respected if they are more obviously stuck forever in their current rut. Even if it's a successful rut. Those women may be great, but they'll never change again, while the rest of us claim the ability to reinvent ourselves infinitely, in the way only men used to. Now women can be dicks, as well. If feminism couldn't humanize your gender, it at least gave us the tools to despise you all equally, in turn. We'll take it, you know?

"And it's not an infinite hate. Not all the way down to the soul of each man. It's just a surface hostility—the same hostility that men have been lazily superimposing, without prejudice or distinction, on the women in their lives for centuries. You: you're pretty enough, of course," she told him as he worked to make her cum again. "But otherwise, you're pretty interchangeable. It's not as though your quality as a sex partner is totally unique, hate to break it to you. I mean, you're good at giving oral, obviously."

She looked at his bare back. It was ornamented with muscles, which made him look invincible. But then every occasional intake of air into his lungs made him look vulnerable. Underneath his rock-hard exoskeleton, he was gas and air and puncturable organs, just like everyone else.

"Our ambivalence about the role of creation in our own lives, our fear of it, can be heard in the way we talk about cultural production, too," she said. "Witness how all forms of art have been demoted to the catch-all noun of 'content.' The real story now—the real Eros—is how we get the content: is it streamed? Coaxial cable? Is it viewed on a tablet? Talk that talk. That's what's sexy. The celebratory unveiling of a new range of offerings by a device manufacturer is our new Oscars. Business stories are what inspire lust, not Arts review sections."

She took a few deep breaths before continuing. "Let's make a list of the ridiculous words they still use in book reviews today, despite the fact that no one thinks of books as exhibiting these functions: 'boundary-breaking,' 'shattering,' 'original,' 'transformative.' All these empowered descriptors—they date from a prior America. One that could be influenced by abstractions on a page. Only 40 years ago, a book could ruin a president; today we can know everything about how the world does business, be outraged by the knowledge, and still not be in a position to change anything.

"Now the only honorable position is to detest all these decadent, pretend responses to art," she said, grinding out her next orgasm on the intern's smooth chin. "The accolades all feel counterfeit. They are impersonating the hosannas of decades past."

After her outburst-and-orgasm in the car, Crissy's thoughts turned, with no small self-satisfaction, to the ex-wives of politically ambitious billionaires—and how they really ought to be more careful with their charity-ball drunk talk. Only one in a hundred media-socialite ladies among their mutual acquaintances might have decoded the meaning behind Ms. Corinne Testington-Marglaze's veiled reference to the "dead girl or live boy" maxim regarding an office seeker's electability. Most of the other ladies at the fund-raiser had thought that Corinne was suggesting—how absolutely delicious of her!—that her ex-husband, Dennett Meyerbeer, might be, at minimum, bisexual.

But unfortunately for the man who was rumored to be exploring a U.S. Senate bid on the Democratic ticket, Crissy had been there too—the one among a hundred who had recognized that there was more than one kind of live boy. As in: another male child, springing from some other union. The sort of live boy about whom even a wildly successful divorcée like Corinne might still feel raw, all these years later. Crissy's father had been loath to confirm that she was right, much less thank her. But the attentions of the intern and the smooth ride home to her well-appointed West Village apartment were universal thanks enough, at least for the moment.

"Arrrmphh," Crissy said, flexing her ankles and gripping the far side of the backseat with her right hand.

"Hey, Crissy," the intern dared to say, after pulling up his head from between her legs. "That's not a word."

Might have to learn this one's name, she thought.

CHAPTER SEVEN:

CAMP ECHO WARDEN'S CHAMBERS,
GAZA, WYOMING
THURSDAY, AUGUST 6, 2015, 2:00 A.M. (MOUNTAIN TIME)

The wiry and fit Warden Lovegren now demanded a hundred push-ups of himself. He was hoping that the repeated dips and rises would bring on a state of post-exertion fatigue. For in these very late hours, the warden—who prided himself on maintaining an unflappable manner, even in moments of great extremity—felt like checking a mirror to confirm that his face was not actually turning some new rage-tinted color. He thought about calling that Democratic Party operative back and screaming into his ear for the better part of an hour—or however long it might take to regain an even-keeled mood.

It's probably nothing. That's what the wuss-voiced Democratic dope had said, wasn't it? Purest hokum. A blast in the women's barracks tonight had become the first black mark against Lovegren's security record in the half year since he had gained command of the camp. He could count on a visit from a three-star general before the week was out. And not long after that, the CIA would surely wave in some hard-looking, no-questions-answering types who would ride around the camp in their freshly armored SUVs for a look-see while ignoring and probably insulting Lovegren's staff.

The holy amount of hell tonight's explosion was about to rain down on the warden's life was simply unacceptable—all the more because he had, after all, been goddamned right about the locus of the trouble. He had nearly wanted to swallow his pistol after reading, in the Incidence of Unsanctioned Violence report, that the ex-journalist had set off the blast. Lovegren was sure she, and her senseless detonation, were connected to the Democratic operative's faux-innocent questioning about a "notable" Palestinian refugee lodged somewhere in New Gaza. But how, exactly?

Before Lovegren bawled out the Democrat, he'd quiz the lady bomber. Already the warden knew the odds were not in favor of his somehow falling back asleep this evening. Not after that alarm had rung in the hallway outside his bedroom. And surely not after his first squinting review of the preliminary report on the explosion and its subsequent fires, here in the camp that he oversaw and remained adamant about residing in (unlike some among his managerial cohort, who lived outside the encampments they oversaw). Lovegren would be awake until dawn. Fucking politics. It could still end Lovegren's career, despite his decades of faithful and efficient service.

The newly touch-and-go status of Lovegren's role as proconsul of New Gaza started to wear on him even more as he walked down the hallway connecting his personal chambers to his office. Upon arrival, he at last set eyes on the woman bomber. Her presence proved even more unsettling than her attack on the camp, not least because she had somehow charmed Lovegren's bureaucratic underlings in the quarter of an hour that she had been stationed outside his office. When the door opened and the woman was shown in—newly shackled at the wrists, waist and feet

84

—she was concluding some bit of private humor with the soldier who led her through the shuffle-foot paces necessary to bring her in front of Lovegren's desk.

Though a touch on the heavy side, the lady bomber (and sometime journalist) was still attractive, Lovegren decided with a lordly air. And not all beautiful women had her same degree of dominion over their naturally bestowed gifts. Right away, the warden could see how her interaction with the serviceman merely hinted at the power she controlled. Lovegren squinted at the private first class as if to say, "Good God, man: soldier up." The subordinate took the point and awkwardly choked off the convivial mood he had been tricked into sharing with the prisoner. Already the warden was getting a pain in his right eyeball socket.

The woman was seated in front of him now. Calm. Assured. It spooked Lovegren, who longed in these moments for the day of paper filing systems. What he would have given to rifle through a manila folder or two while beginning his questioning, the better to pretend that the issue was not sufficiently serious to command his whole attention. Lovegren could have scrolled through the Incidence of Unsanctioned Violence memo on his phone, but for all the prisoner knew, he could have been texting a paramour.

Fuck it all to hell, Lovegren thought—she must know she's the star of the hour. Nothing to be done about that. Might as well begin.

"Philomela," he started, sounding out the syllables in an earnest, slow fashion that indicated, instead of a problem with phonetic word attack, the warden's intention to insult and intimidate the prisoner.

She seemed neither intimidated nor insulted. "You can call me Melly," she replied. "Everyone who knows me does."

By suggesting imminent familiarity, was she tipping her hand? Did she think that the warden, like the grunt outside the door, could be so easily made to purr in her lap? She certainly had a stylish way with a blunt opening move, this mad lady bomber (Lovegren had decided to start calling her this, at least to himself, since her motivations were still obscure enough to qualify as potentially insane).

"No—I don't think we'll be friends straight away," he said, fixing Melly in his gaze. If he couldn't distract himself with paperwork, the next best thing was to bear down on her with all available intensity.

Melly faced up to the warden's staring and, realizing that he could not be charmed directly, changed tactics. In a moment, her posture stiffened. Her face dimmed from friendly to businesslike— the kind of mien often employed just before the conversational gambit "Now I'm sure you're a busy man, so I won't waste your time."

"Warden Lovegren," Melly said with utmost respect. "I know I have committed a serious infraction; I won't pretend I haven't."

He guffawed angrily. "How generous of you!"

"But think beyond the shock of the incident itself, and the minor downgrade to your security rating," Melly continued. "Was anyone killed in the blast? No. Did I attempt to evade or mislead the security officers in my cell block? If you look again at the report you've doubtless already read four times over, you'll notice that I did not." The warden watched Melly attempt half a smile. A conspiratorial, let's-be-reasonable twist to her face.

"So you'd like a parade, then?" Lovegren said, realizing as soon as he'd said this that his sarcasm amounted to a giveaway. The mad lady bomber had gotten under his skin in, what, under five minutes?

"No," Melly said, daring to smile even more broadly. "I'd like you to ask the question you'd ask of any rational actor in this situation—presuming you think I've met the standard of 'rational,' which I'd like to think I have."

"OK then, Philomela. Why in heaven's name did you blow up your empty cell this evening?"

The maybe-not-so-mad bomber lubricated her throat with a small swallow of saliva, as though she wanted to make sure her voice would not crack while delivering the next line in her well-rehearsed script. "Because, Warden: You have a political problem brewing here. And because I wager that I'm the first to have identified it, I figured it was in your long-term interest that I find the fastest possible way to tell you."

"So you detonated an improvised explosive device."

"Another way of looking at it," Melly countered, "is that I'm here talking to you within a day of realizing that a future candidate for the United States Senate has an illegitimate son who resides here in New Gaza."

Warden Lovegren sucked in his cheeks and squinted at the jailed reporter.

"I've said something interesting, haven't I?"

For the next half hour, the warden demanded that the presumptuous prisoner show her work—that she spell out the deductive logic behind what would appear, on its face, to be a rather far-fetched claim. But even as he put Melly through her evidentiary paces, Lovegren knew she was correct about one thing: perhaps more than a few people suspected that a potential Democratic candidate for Senate might have an illegitimate Palestinian child living in the camp. The warden assumed it was this suspicion that had prompted the night's impertinent call from Beverly Steindler. The Democratic party's operators must have been investigating the would-be senator's background. They probably wanted to see if even the faintest whiff of knowledge regarding the boy's parentage had wafted up to the highest levels of New Gaza's administration. *The blood-sucking politicos could have at least done their parasitic work during normal business hours,* Lovegren thought to himself as Melly prattled on, so very proud of her dot-connecting work.

He didn't particularly need to hear how, when working at a national newsweekly, Melly had chanced to hear several lectures by the venture-capital titan Dennett Meyerbeer (whose dalliances as a part-time press baron were well known). At first, the fact that the writer-turned-prisoner would know Mr. Meyerbeer's face well enough to recognize its likeness in a child seemed a riotously unfair piece of bad luck for the warden. But then again, reporters were always in possession of inconvenient knowledge, and even the most dedicated reader of a particular writer's byline had no earthly way of knowing the scope of a journalist's as-yet-unpublished hunches. In this case, an erstwhile employer of Melly's had tasked her with performing a background check on the adult Meyerbeer in the run-up to his acquisition of a stake in the publication.

Thus Melly knew that Meyerbeer had made his first small fortune as part of a French-Saudi investment consortium—one skilled enough to suck up a plurality of the development contracts in downtown Beirut's commercial area during the first flowering of commerce in the years after Lebanon's civil war. Meyerbeer had maintained two residences in Beirut: one on the Muslim-dominated west side of town, where he conducted official business, the other on the Christian-coded east side. When his assets came under scrutiny during the acquisition of Melly's employer, the finance wizard never offered an explanation for this complicated multiple-domicile arrangement.

"Even if I hadn't been tasked with doing a data dive on the personal files that Meyerbeer's assistants provided to the company, I would have heard him waxing neoliberal about the New Beirut of the Rafik Hariri era in one of his public addresses to the staff," Melly told the warden. "He loved to talk about his experience. Even then he was rumored to be a potential senatorial candidate."

"And what makes you think he's running for Senate now?" Lovegren finally asked, interrupting her monologue.

"I didn't know that he was," Melly said. "Until you kept listening to me instead of throwing me in solitary confinement." The pain behind the warden's right eye socket had grown to a sufficient level that it now merited a five-second application of pressure from his right palm. Would it help his cause if he were to swear to the mad lady bomber that he did not, as it happened, know for certain that Mr. Meyerbeer would leap into the 2016 election cycle? All he did know was that Democratic operatives in Washington were intent on interrupting his sleep.

But the ex-journalist had already sped around that bend. "The dates fit," she said with exclamatory emphasis. "A child conceived in Lebanon, post–civil war, around 1997 or so, would be 18 years old today. The boy I saw preparing stand-up for tonight's —sorry, last night's—under-20 youth event, that's him. He looked well brought up. And then—I mean, that nose. You'd recognize it anywhere. Then I heard him making indignant reference to the American businessmen who profited during the revitalization of downtown Beirut.

"If it only took me the better part of an evening to process this fact pattern, you have to wonder, Warden Lovegren: how much longer do you have before this camp gets turned upside-fucking-down with some multitent media circus? A Senate candidate confronted with questions of parentage—maybe he turns the tables by becoming a Palestinian rights activist. Demands access to his son? And then you've got demonstrators at your gates. From both parties. Plus independents. Then maybe some more civilian rockets get shot into the camp. How long do you have to think about your options, in terms of skirting just such an outcome? How long before you need my help? You see, there wasn't any time to waste."

Lovegren's posture gave up trying to confront the events of the day. He crumpled in his seat. There was no further point in trying to match his pride against that of his prisoner. She had the cards; the Furies had decreed that Lovegren was going to be batted around by political developments. All that remained was to figure out what might possibly be done to minimize the damage.

That a onetime journalist was encouraging him to tap her expertise on outflanking the press was not nothing, either.

"I hope you'll appreciate my discretion in not asking how it is that you know about Meyerbeer's plans," Melly continued, as if trying to offer him a modicum of comfort.

"I do appreciate that," the warden said. After a minute, he added: "I presume you have another proposal handy."

"Just so."

"Does it involve a goodly amount of explosives?"

"Not so goodly," Melly answered, with more than a little charm.

Lying in bed later that night, Lovegren considered the conversation he had had with Philomela in its entirety. Lovegren did not think himself a vain man; he was conscious that the most impressive years of his physical beauty were behind him, no matter his exercise regimen. Yet he was still slightly embarrassed to have appeared feckless in front of such a capable woman. He might still need to fire someone in the security detail for not spotting the sale of explosives in the women's barracks—but if that's what he decided to do, he hoped it wouldn't be out of a misplaced desire to prove his potency.

He next wondered whether he might one day be glad to have known this woman, with the ridiculous name that he dimly recognized from his old AP Greek-mythology courses. Should any parent, Lovegren thought, ever be humorously vindictive enough to want to steer a child into the singularly drab and arrogance-perfumed halls of journalism, they could do worse than give a child a pretentious name from antiquity. Good Lord! She had been fated to become fucked, more or less.

The story of the original Philomela of mythology went that she had been raped and then had her tongue carved out to prevent her from speaking of the crime. What a name this journalist-turned-prisoner had been carrying around for 30-odd years! Despite her imprisonment—banishment, really—in the finest imitation of old czarist Siberia that her own country had ever devised, and despite the ever-disappearing profit margins of her profession and its subsequent degraded march into the muck of compromise, Philomela retained the sense of entitled pride that had yet to be snuffed out of journalism's more stalwart practitioners; Lovegren had seen that as soon as she had entered his receiving chambers.

For Philomela Shroud—though clearly well possessed of the understanding that she was in a bad way—had still managed to appear, to the warden, duly impressed with herself. Or perhaps more accurately, she had looked proud of the story she had found and was chasing. She wanted to break a story tonight: that was the best way to understand her, the warden thought, lying back once again in bed. Tonight, in lieu of an editor or readers, her audience had been Lovegren. She was probably an excellent reporter, the warden decided.

Lovegren needed to pursue a new line of thought if he was to massage his mind into a rhythm not wholly hostile to sleep. Hadn't he suppressed all sorts of attacks in his first months supervising Camp Echo? Yes, he had. But the warden knew that the price of success was jealousy; others would be quick to find his achievement short-lived. Even a small explosion could be used to gainsay his past and present efforts. "Ah, but Lovegren tamped down the violence in his camp for only a season" or the like would pass between the more senior wardens of nearby encampments. He had to do something about it, and publicly. Lovegren considered inviting a journalist from the outside to come witness the cold effectiveness of his response.

The only question was how many layers of fiction would go into the public theatrics related to securing the camp. Lovegren had turned pale when Philomela suggested, as a remedy, that she might stage another blast in the coming week to aid with her proposed plan. That she herself wanted to escape was clear enough; she had admitted to fear of serial rape. At that point in their discussion Warden Lovegren had privately berated himself, because he could not scoff at Philomela on this count. He knew rape to be a systemic problem in the medium-security blocks reserved for non-debtor prisoners. He hated that this was the case, and had yet to engineer a satisfactory remedy.

But sympathizing with Philomela's plight was not the same as trusting her. She had asked the warden to hire her for a covert assignment: the spiriting of Meyerbeer's illegitimate son away from New Gaza. With Lovegren's blessing, she would watch over and supervise the child for as long as Meyerbeer's candidacy remained viable. Philomela had proposed reporting to Lovegren via hand-to-hand intel-passing back channels. No email or phones. And then, once Meyerbeer's candidacy had finished one way or another—and rendered the illegitimate son's parentage moot to the press—a "capture" of the "missing" prisoners could be arranged. At that point, if Lovegren was of a suitably lenient mind, he might recommend Philomela's early release.

This was an intriguingly inventive head fake. If Democratic operatives came to the camp in search of the boy—and it was more a matter of when, rather than if—the warden might plausibly admit no knowledge of the youngster's whereabouts. The scary part was that it could even possibly be true. Once out in the free world, Philomela might be smart enough to keep her location, and the boy's, secret even from him.

Given all the particulars that needed turning over, was it a surprise that Lovegren was still no closer to sleep? Tossing in his bed, in the next room over from where he'd first lain eyes on a journalist condemned by the Patriot Act, the warden wondered whether she ever considered her mythic forerunner.

"Melly," the warden said quietly, allowing himself for the first time to shorten her name as she had suggested when first trying to win him over. The warden knew two things in this moment: that he was thinking of accepting her plan, and that he shouldn't bother trying to get any shut-eye. That convergence led him to the understanding that there would be no better time to put Philomela's plan into action than now, before the Democrats sent whomever it was they would be sending.

He rose from the bed and began drafting an email to his deputy, Mr. Clamp. The subject line: "Jailbreak." And then, in a flash, the warden saw himself testifying before Congress. Subpoenaed inboxes could be a problem. Should he delete the message-in-progress? Was this a task unfit for interoffice email? He was too tired to be paranoid. In the body of the email he requested Mr. Clamp's immediate presence, then clicked "Send." If Lovegren could not sleep, why should his deputy? After all, if they were going to put Philomela to work, it was better to start right away, before too many people would be able to notice that she had ever stayed in Camp Echo at all.

CHAPTER EIGHT:

CAMP ECHO SUB-21 ORPHAN BLOCK,
GAZA, WYOMING
THURSDAY, AUGUST 6, 2015, 4:00 A.M. (MOUNTAIN TIME)

Ghassan Khouri sat alert in his cell, upright on the bottom bunk, waiting for a chance to debrief with the friendliest guard in the Palestinian orphan barracks. His dude Howard had shown up at the public tent for Gus's stand-up act that evening. The boy was impatient to hear the inevitable review, though he knew that Howard, a 6'8" verified Choctaw under U.S.-citizen lockdown, could only come around to chew the fat after finishing his nightly rounds in the building. Well after lights-out, they would have to whisper through the bar-covered square placed at chin height in the otherwise solid-metal cell door, Howard scrunching his neck to make his voice heard.

Gus's cellmate—a broody, uninteresting jock named Danny—had a cranky older person's way of insisting on a proper night's sleep; when Gus and Howard occasionally got too loud during their after-hours commiserations, Danny would threaten to report Howard's friendly nature to the meanest-possible inmate supervisor in Camp Echo. Sometimes Gus worried about graduating out of the youth barracks—a reality staring him down, with just under 30 months to go—but the chance to leave the 17-year-old Danny behind was not one of the changes that gave him the sweats. They'd been picked, like most Palestinian-orphan cellmate dyads were, on the basis of their vestigial religious affiliation—both Gus and Danny had been raised in at least nominally Christian households, supposedly reducing the odds of friction between them—but that was pretty much where the camp's cellmate suitability profiling had concluded.

While Danny snored away, Gus reflected on his 15 minutes in front of the crowd tonight. His principal takeaway was that it had come off fine, all things considered. One family had seemed impatient with Gus's unrelenting sarcasm, as they were waiting to hear their 12-year-old daughter's take on some traditional Syrian fiddling motifs. Some of the older Palestinian residents had whistled in response to the stray scraps of vulgarity that the teen had allowed himself as a form of punctuation.

With these older folks, Gus suspected that his cynicism hadn't been the problem. Any Palestinian refugee who had made the transfer across continents—from an out-of-the-way shithole camp in the Levant to a less shitty one in Wyoming—was certainly on familiar terms with the absurd. It was just the swearing they couldn't cotton to. But cursing was what American comics did. And even though Ghassan Khouri knew that a serious interval would likely elapse between now and the time that any professional U.S. comedian would be able to hear his material, the boy was already taking his desired future audience's preferences into account. The camp elders would just have to fucking deal, Gus thought.

A few minutes after 4 a.m., Howard peered through the barred, square hole of the door into Gus and Danny's room. "Khouri, get your ass over here," he said with mock-stentorian severity, a parody of an asshole guard. Danny moaned a small protest from the upper bunk as Gus sprang with light-footed alacrity from his bed.

Howard gave a short, quiet whistle, peering inside Gus's room. "It never gets old," he began, "comparing this place to the rez. The hookup you have here is, like, truly beyond what your average Choctaw would even be prepared to believe, if I could go and tell them what goes on 'round these parts."

"Said the guard *into* the cell full of reinforced steel."

"Ah, that's just for the wee orphans' protection. Making sure the bigger ones among you don't terrorize the runts. You seen the palaces that proper families get here? The teachers for your schools? Let me go run up 30-thou in credit-card debt—and then sign me up for this kind of debtors' prison, you know?"

"So this is a be-thankful-for-what-you-have sort of chat?"

Howard cracked a high-pitched but formidable laugh that Gus could feel through the floor. "Oh, everywhere I go, I'm bringing the gospel of thankfulness to any of those with the good fortune not to hail from the land I call home," Howard started. "But rest easy, boss: we're gonna talk about your jokes tonight too."

"Shut the fuck up, *en jad*," Danny hissed from the top bunk.

"What did you think?" Gus whispered even more quietly, but with additional impatience.

"Brother—," Howard began. At this precise moment, the evening's second blooming cloud of deepest-timbre rumble—and another wave of cracking concrete and airborne paperwork—swallowed up the rest of the guard's sentence, as well as everything else in the nearby sonic field. They were very near to the explosion. Gus instinctively twisted his neck for a view down the hall beyond his cell, but being nearly flush with the door already, all he could see was Howard's departure: the tall guard waved at Gus with one trailing hand as the other reached for a holstered Taser.

"Fuckin' hell," Danny said from the top bunk, pulling a pillow down hard over his ears just as the din started to fade.

"Remember, this explosion is just, like, some random shit," Gus said, turning away from the door while needling his roommate. "If you're gonna be a bitch and keep records about after-hours noise, at least be fair about it. This one isn't on me."

Then Gus heard the voice of a woman—quite a foreign sound in the boys' block—directly behind his head. "Ghassan Khouri?" it asked.

"Um, yes?" he replied. As he did, he immediately recognized the woman from that afternoon's mic check. She had been "supervising," or whatever they called what the U.S. convicts did when they were hanging around with their walkie-talkies.

"This is actually just the tiniest bit about you, son."

Then Ghassan heard the lock in his door turning.

CHAPTER NINE:

CHILTON MEYERBEER RESIDENCE,
WEST HOLLYWOOD, CALIFORNIA
THURSDAY, AUGUST 6, 2015, 11:15 A.M. (PACIFIC TIME)

After reading Beverly's file, Persia had moved quickly to arrive at the door of hir new assignment's living quarters by the following morning. Ze thought it would have taken longer—given how the rural, two-runway Wyoming airport hadn't featured direct flights into LAX, and how ze'd needed to suffer a prop plane into Seattle-Tacoma—but the transfers were slick; there had been no delays. Ze would have preferred to ambush young Meyerbeer in the late afternoon, as it was always best to surprise the rich and idle just as the flimsy seal against slightly-too-early cocktails was being broken. But ze'd take an 11 a.m. stroll through West Hollywood, heat and all.

At least now ze was in Los Angeles, which wasn't nothing. Inveigh against it as much as you wanted—and Persia hirself did, plenty—but upon entry to the city's spritzy, welcoming atmosphere, it was difficult not to feel newly birthed. It was damn near foamy even on the smoggiest of days, and the mild vibe of the metropolis was, for Persia, only barely dampened by its status as a holy land of American automotive culture. If most of the Angelenos that Persia had ever carpooled with were grade-A complainers about traffic, they also loved the unhurried opportunity to scope out the acquisitive choices made by their gridlocked neighbors, an act never better undertaken than in static, close proximity to the vehicles of others.

Even after granting as sensible the attention paid to horsepower in this town, Persia found the large, winding path that led from the palm-tree-festooned, impossibly wide West Hollywood avenue up to Chilton Meyerbeer's hillside manse to be something else indeed. Cars were everywhere, ditched along the never-ending driveway in an efficiency-blind manner reminiscent of the way spoiled children deposit toys throughout an undisciplined house. Lock the gate, strip the many houseguests of their keys, and the young Meyerbeer could have himself a rather ripping little used-car lot, in the event that he needed some side money. Not that he ever would.

Was this a party? So early in the morning? Or had last night's festivities not yet reached their coke-addled conclusion? Persia shuddered and began psyching hirself up for a late morning of full-on social pretending. It was necessary to prepare in this fashion, given that the breezy nonchalance required of all party crashers was not an attitude that the Democratic Senatorial Campaign Committee's top investigator could generate on command. Persia, in a party setting, often found hirself at war with an impulse to flip over the appetizer plate, then melt down in private. Ze didn't do groups; ze wasn't a fund-raiser, out throwing bashes to raise money for the committee. There was a reason Beverly had given Persia the task of sitting eyeball to eyeball across a table from one person at a time.

As ze walked up the hill-ish drive toward the white, villa-like main residence that could now be perceived farther ahead, Persia realized that, in terms of hir phobia regarding large gatherings, ze seemed to be lucking out. Upon reaching an enclosure of greenery —a semi-private area abutting the hillside footpath, bound by manicured, shoulder-height shrubbery—Persia saw that it wasn't a party ze should prepare to interrupt.

A teary-eyed violinist of French extraction (if Persia had to guess) was sitting on one of the elegantly sculpted marble benches within the hedge-bounded area. She looked at Persia but said nothing straight away, and did not bother to turn her head all the way around to face the interloper. The violinist was gripping her instrument by its neck—the body of the elegantly burnished item ever so slightly swinging in the musician's right hand, almost coming into contact with both the marble bench's edge and the ground beneath it. Persia was not an expert on instruments, but it didn't seem the right way to treat an obviously expensive item; every part of it, including the finish of the wood, seemed vulnerable when compared with the unforgiving hardness of earth and lawn sculpture alike.

"You're not my replacement? Not so fast, already, like finger-snap-done?" the woman asked. She turned her whole face toward Persia, who, at the same time, was considering whether or not to lie to the violinist, the better to soak up the information behind her question more quickly.

But, not counting on hirself to keep up the ruse for very long —and thinking that the woman would prove better as a trusting confessor than as an immediately-lied-to acquaintance—Persia opted for honesty. "Nope," ze said.

"Right," the violinist replied, addressing a running nostril with both a slurping half-inhale and a swipe underneath the nose with a tissue clenched in the hand not gripping her instrument.

"Because, first off, that's too fast, even for Chilton. And second: I've never seen you, plus where's even your instrument, et cetera." Her long black hair was slick-straight and rigorously parted down the middle, framing some daringly hot-pink lipstick that threatened to infantilize the woman's overall palette, yet did not. Persia thought she was a stunner—even if she was not hir type. (Or even a candidate for later obsessing.) The look was too broad, inviting too many potential applicants. Hers was a mainstream perfection.

"So: what are you doing here?" the woman said. "You're not screwing Chilton, either. And those are, like, the two categories for women in his life: performers and fuck-n-suck pals. Trust me. I've been both."

Persia found hirself stopped a bit dumb. "Well, you're right about most of that," ze said after a pause. "I'm not fucking Chilton. Not that I expect it would be of interest to either one of us."

"L-O-L," the violinist said, spelling out each letter. "You're better off."

Persia smiled sympathetically.

"But as for my question," the violinist continued, as though reminding herself that she shouldn't trust Persia so quickly, "if you're not here to rehearse his music or sleep in his bed—maybe go ahead and state your business."

"Didn't realize you were the bouncer."

"Just giving you a chance to practice your opening lines," the violinist replied with a trace of hardness in her voice. Then, as though wanting to add back a touch of sweetness, she said: "You'll see we're all about practice around here. Suggest anything beyond that, get ready to get murked."

Persia didn't recognize the word "murked," but wasn't in the habit of telegraphing hir lexicographical ignorance, especially when the meaning was clear enough from context. Beverly's file hadn't fully prepared hir for the strange route ze was taking to the house—that much was clear. Ze figured ze might as well come out with something resembling the naked truth.

"Fact is, I'm an investigator."

"Government jacket, or more the private style?"

"Depends how you look at it."

"Oh, girl," the violinist said, rising from the marble bench and striding over to Persia as part of her exit from the private-feeling arena. "I don't have *to do* with politics. I'm gonna go ahead and get up out of here."

Persia stopped breathing for a second as the beautiful stranger passed hir near the break in the shrubbery. The woman had taken three strides away before Persia hollered: "How is it you peg me as a girl?"

"Oh I know what's up," the violinist said. "My cuz is genderqueer like that. I just don't have time to figure it all out. Like, I'm sure there's articles or books that could help me know how to not misgender you or whatever. But it's not my thing. Music comes first."

Persia was just barely keeping pace with the violinist's chosen argot of abbreviation. Everything about the woman—her cut-and-dried, know-it-all air, as well as the relentlessly intense focus on casual diction—was making hir upset.

"And your cousin," Persia said, finally, to the girl's back. "Totally cool with your disregarding the points outside the gender binary? Like, do you just call your cousin 'girl' too?"

"He's really a boy," the woman said, throwing up a dismissive wave of the right hand. She was still walking away from Persia, still gripping her instrument with her left hand. Then, in the hand held aloft, she raised a middle finger, disappearing down the hill to her car. "I told you—just like I told Chil'—I don't fuck with politics."

Every ten feet or so, as Persia strode uphill to young Meyerbeer's house, ze kept expecting a glass shield to shoot up out of the ground in front of hir. But, just as there had been no gate at the foot of the hill, neither did there seem to be any security system in place beyond the front door itself. Persia rang the intercom buzzer and immediately heard a sensual but sharply robotic, feminine voice phonetically sounding out the phrase: "Sorry, no admittance can be granted at this time."

The recording was clipped, but not unfriendly. "A rehearsal is in progress for another. Forty. Three. Minutes," it continued, halting ever so slightly as its controlling software fed it the correct information. "Please ring again later." Persia pressed hir ear against the white door, finished to a lacquered shine that also preserved the contrail-like sweeps of wood grain underneath. The house was much like that all over: stucco surface affectations suggesting an ad-hoc, self-styled approach to groovy filigree, appended to a form of architecture that was more solidly moneyed, in an old-world way.

Persia waited. Ze was prepared to give this another 43 minutes. Mostly, ze was curious to find out whether the robotic doorbell/answering service was an elaborate brush-off. Would it just kick the scheduling can down the road, and propose a new interval of time after this countdown was complete? Even if it did, Persia decided ze could use at least some portion of the next hour to calm down, after hir collision with the violinist.

It was often the people who could claim glancing familiarity with genderqueer issues who felt most comfortable taking egregious liberties. These people assumed more. Presumed things to a degree you wouldn't think possible from someone who had witnessed a loved one make some difficult calls. It was infuriating, but also understandable in its all-too-human way: when presented with odd-looking data that seemed to not fit inside life's most familiar patterns, many felt the need to jam it into place, like a stubbornly unusable jigsaw puzzle piece. Persia had seen this in the realm of politics—with individuals making veritable full-time jobs out of ignoring the complexity of facts sitting in front of their faces. Why wouldn't that trait have purchase in the broader world, as well?

Persia pressed the doorbell again. The robot voice responded that a reply could not be expected for another. Twenty. Two. Minutes. Ze checked the countdown's progress against the time on hir phone. The doorbell was sticking to its story, at any rate. Persia thought for a moment about rifling through Beverly's file on the Meyerbeer clan one more time, but decided against it; ze more or less had the whole thing memorized. What Persia really needed now was to meet this family's junior-most member (according to the official record).

Just as Persia was about to buzz the doorbell again— according to hir phone, the 43 minutes had now passed—ze heard a rustling from within. Before ze had a chance to secure hir overnight suitcase or hir messenger bag, much less plant hir feet on the marble steps, both halves of the egress swung out on their hinges. A torrent of mostly young musicians spilled from the house, speaking a shared language of exhaustion, instruments slung over shoulders in hard-plastic protective casings.

"Good God, fresh air."

"How often you think he comes outside and feels it?"

There must have been about three dozen players. The few who took more than a moment's notice of Persia looked surprised to encounter hir on the other side of the door. Ze knew that this stunned reaction might not have been due to hir idiosyncratic mien, but rather the relative rarity of petitioners walking right up to Chilton Meyerbeer's house.

"Is Mr. Meyerbeer in?" Persia asked one of the members of this group, a mid-twenties-looking black man who was gingerly navigating a double bass—perched on what looked like a single wheel belonging to a child's toy—down the hard but slick front steps.

"Rehearsal's over, in case you're one of the singers who didn't show. I wouldn't go in there."

"Uh, no—I don't—I mean, that wouldn't be me," Persia said, just as it seemed the bass player had taken enough notice of hir face that he could now add a quizzical twist to his own. "Do you know if he has a scheduler I might speak to, or—"

"There's no staff here...," the bass player said, with a syntactic space left for an additional word that he, thankfully, gave no voice to. *Lady*, perhaps. Persia tried to show with hir eyebrows how grateful ze was for the man's circumspect avoidance of gender, but wasn't sure that ze'd yet perfected such communicative subtlety with any of the follicles on hir body.

"You can go right in, I guess," the bass player added as he guided his instrument from the final step to the drought-arid soil. "Take the stairway off the main foyer down to the underground studio. He'll probably be wrapping cables for the better part of an hour."

Persia raised an arm as if to wish the bass player safe travels down the hill with his ungainly instrument, but he didn't seem to be looking back for any gestural pleasantries. Persia was also taking stock of the dryness of manner exhibited by most of the exiting instrumentalists. Even the violinist, who had originally presented herself as friendly and expansive, had turned miserly with information, as though remembering a dictum of the grounds.

The musicians seemed to feel quite comfortable speaking of Chilton with a candor bordering on derision. Persia understood that they were his employees; as such, maintaining a certain critical detachment was their capitalistic purview. Still, even the most unbecoming of bosses tended to require of employees the recitation of a grudgingly respectful script while at the place of transacted labor. As Persia walked inside the empty and therefore slightly spooky foyer, ze decided that either musicians as an employee class were more flagrantly disrespectful of their bosses than most workers were, or that the freedom ze had observed was tolerated, and perhaps even promoted, by young Meyerbeer himself.

A look inside the grand entryway confirmed that the scion was nothing if not willing to indulge the outlandish decorative gesture. The white floors, walls and staircases that spiraled off the hall were lacquered with a clear finish so pure and reflective that Persia thought about fishing out hir sunglasses from the rolling suitcase. As the bass player had indicated, at the rear of the foyer, another marble staircase descended to a basement level. Each side of its narrow passageway was covered in a large-format rendering of an archival black-and-white photo.

Both photographs were of men seated in front of pianos, and though they were taken at different angles, both musicians' gazes seemed directed right at whoever was walking down the stairs. Persia did not recognize either man. The one covering the entire left wall was a large, black middle-aged man in a 1940s suit, an anarchically overstuffed and ready-to-fall-apart cigarette dangling from his lower lip. He was looking up at the photographer's lens; pages of musical notation were visible on the piano's music stand, which framed the man's left shoulder. He looked tired but triumphant, Persia thought.

Facing hir from the right side was a youthful white player, captured in profile while sitting at his piano, wearing a denim shirt that also looked like a product of the 1940s. His hair appeared to be of the flaxen blond variety, and was long enough to be tucked behind the ear. And while the smile on his face had obviously been directed at an out-of-frame intimate, it seemed, from the vantage of the staircase, that he could be gazing up and welcoming Persia to the mansion's lower level.

At the bottom of the staircase, Persia discerned another function of the black-and-white photographs: they were a bridge between the bright whiteness of the rest of the house and this basement level, which was floored and paneled in near-complete blackness. A series of small recording booths was divided by glass partitions and lined with black foam soundproofing material. The carpeting was constructed from a braid of thick black and gray fibers, which proved spookily able to absorb and erase Persia's footfalls.

This step-by-step silence meant that when Persia came upon the hunched, seated figure of what ze guessed to be Chilton Meyerbeer—the only human presence in a large recording studio otherwise filled by several dozen folding chairs and music stands— hir approach took the form of a well-executed ambush, much to the surprise of Persia hirself. Ze had all but assumed, having rung the doorbell at several points within the last hour, that hir advance upon the house had been well telegraphed. But, since the bass player had apparently been truthful when relaying that Meyerbeer had no full-time staff, Persia stalled in the studio's doorway for a moment, unsure how to begin.

Sensing hir presence, Chilton turned around—at first with the fear of a man who has already spent more than a moment or two thinking about home invasion.

"There's no cash...," he started, before estimating the odds of Persia being a thief as relatively low. He looked something like the white piano player whose portrait graced the right-hand stairway wall. But the resemblance might have rested mostly on Chilton's shoulder-length blond hair. He certainly did not favor his balding father; Persia made a mental note to re-check the photos of Corinne Testington-Marglaze to see if there was a likeness on that side of the gene pool.

To hir relief, Chilton did not evince either of the two principal reactions that assholes exhibited upon first meeting hir.

He did not perform a gratuitous double take, nor did he make a great show of avoiding eye contact after taking in hir appearance. Instead, Chilton was simply staring at Persia with a not-indifferent coolness. The clarity of his gaze almost made hir forget to state hir business.

"So if you're not here to rob me...," Chilton helpfully prodded, apparently not much inclined to get up from his chair and greet the interloper.

"I have a few questions about your father."

"Not interested," the composer said, continuing to wrap audio cables around his left arm.

"OK, how about your brother, then? Interested in talking about him?"

Chilton Meyerbeer looked up. He started to say something, then paused. He was rethinking his next move, Persia sensed. "Don't have a brother," he said.

"You mean to say you don't *know* your brother, surely," Persia said, slowly walking into the studio. Ze looked at the exotic microphones of varying size, held aloft by black metal stands in semicircular arcs that ringed each empty row of chairs. Setting one knee in a chair two rows from Chilton, ze managed to close the distance between them and remain relatively near the door. Persia needed to keep hir exit-strategy wits about hir, just in case Chilton lashed out at hir provocations.

The composer continued wrapping what Persia assumed were microphone cables. Just as he didn't seem to have any house staff, neither did he seem to employ any assistants or audio engineers. "You seem pretty impressed with yourself," he said.

"Why do you say that?"

"You must love your job," he continued, not really answering hir question. "The way someone walks into a room— sometimes you can really tell how much the job means." Chilton looked up at Persia now. "And if the job confers reputation, then the person just waltzes in, like they own the place. Like you've done, here in my home. Just so you know, I can see that type of thing—and so maybe it's best that you get the fuck out."

Persia was amused. He was talking out of his ass, of course. He hadn't bothered to do any work to figure hir out. And yet his pushback had also unbalanced hir a bit. He'd certainly moved hir off the game plan of teasing him into revealing something about Meyerbeer family life. Now, instead, Persia felt like ze had to defend hir own choices, or respond to the calumny that hir ego was somehow too invested in the particulars of hir career—about which the young composer knew precisely zilch.

"What are you, a venture-capital type, perhaps?" Chilton continued, delicately and precisely twisting the audio cable as though he were caring for an infant. "You want my dad to get in on a round of angel funding? If you think I'm the way into his heart, much less his portfolio, you haven't done your research. You're maybe not as good at your job as you think."

Persia had hir voice back now, and was tired of the lecture. Ze hadn't planned on resorting to the big guns quite so quickly— but this prick had asked for it. "I'm from the Democratic Senatorial Campaign Committee," ze said. "And I have done my research. You hate your father, dislike your mother, and don't think much of the public. Though you do think highly of your own art."

Chilton stopped wrapping audio cables and glanced up at Persia again—this time with what looked like respect.

"So you pay the brightest young Angeleno musicians to come to your house and play your music," Persia continued. "But you don't let anyone hear it outside these walls. You make the players sign nondisclosure agreements before they can take the scores home to practice." Persia held up a torn page from one such document, which ze'd found on the grounds while waiting for the rehearsal to let out. "But you made the mistake of letting your first opera have a premiere—and get covered. And that's why I'm here."

"I regret my dismissive attitude," Chilton said after a pause. And it was no insincere apology; the casual disrespect had been strained from his speech, revealing a capability for genuineness.

Persia softened hir own voice in response to the peace offering in Chilton's new timbre. "I suspect you know that your father has electoral ambitions. Whether he's successful or not isn't up to me—at least not on this trip." Persia looked around the room and wondered, for a moment, how long it had been since Chilton had left his palace.

"So what is your trip about?" he asked.

"Finding out if you really do have a half brother."

It looked as if Chilton might actually start crying, right there and then. "And how do we do that?"

"We find him." Persia didn't know, exactly, where that "we" had come from. Before arriving in Los Angeles, ze'd envisioned this little pop-in visit in more experimental terms. If Chilton Meyerbeer had put up a convincing protest, to the effect that he had no inkling of a half brother, then Persia would have continued on to New Gaza with a greater awareness that this whole thing was a possible dead end. But the topic had clearly struck him with a painful directness.

God help hir, ze wanted to help Chilton. Though ze wasn't quite ready to share the suspicion that ze had already seen his brother.

"You mean, you think you know where he is? Which camp?"

Persia nodded to answer the first question. The second ze didn't answer at all. Persia hoped he wouldn't quite notice. Chilton dropped the audio cables and faced the wall—and when he spoke next, it sounded as though he were confessing to a crime. "Believe me," he said, "I've thought about just rolling up to this or that New Gaza camp. A thousand times."

"They'd have just told you to get your ass back to West Hollywood," Persia said.

"But you can get inside."

"I can't promise that I can get you inside—but if you think you can help, and would like to...," Persia checked the time on hir phone. "Actually, we'd have to scoot to the airport pretty quickly to get a flight and a car into New Gaza before end of business. And you'd have to pay for your own ticket."

At this broaching of workaday practical thinking, the Meyerbeer scion smiled—and Persia thought ze saw the return of a slight arrogance.

Oh, right, ze thought. "You have a private jet, don't you?"

CHAPTER TEN:

JUST DESSERTS RANCH,
UNINCORPORATED COUNTY, WYOMING
THURSDAY, AUGUST 6, 2015, 11:00 A.M. (MOUNTAIN TIME)

Upon parking the camp-issued Lexus, Melly—sporting a new if slightly ill-fitting suit—discovered that the managed-care facility Warden Lovegren had said would be waiting for her and Ghassan was not nearly as grim as she'd imagined. Death's waiting room this wasn't. Instead, it happened to be a luxurious, spa-like oasis, a wonderland for the late-middle-aged and capitalistically successful. Once you got past the armored guards at the perimeter, it was easy to forget there was any strife in the world at all. Ghassan was entranced; Melly presumed he'd never had the creature comforts of the West. He was most likely making a mental queue of the many streaming-media goodies he would be able to access at their new residence.

Melly was less bowled over. In part this was because, back in her days as a free woman, she'd grown blasé about all things swank. Well before her prosecution, she had already become tired of and alienated from the good life—or at least the version experienced and extolled by D.C.-area elites. On the sidelines of her secret court trial (on those rare instances when her lawyers were able to finesse a visit from an associate), Melly's time-limited visitors always seemed to focus on what they perceived as her tragic fall from life's most ideal station. *My God, how did she survive without YogaFlow-on-Dupont?*

True, the incarcerated Melly would have liked to have been able to go to a museum (in New York) or the opera (in Paris)—but she did not miss an existence where a stellar weekend was more or less defined as everyone agreeing that you had looked especially sharp opposite the perma-scowl of George Will on a pundit roundtable. Give her liberty, of course—Free Melly!—but not her former life, precisely.

She did not regret her decision to publish secret documents relating to the proposed administration of the new camps (back when they were still in the planning stages). It was important, Melly had thought, for Americans to realize that the whole contraption would be privatized by the Romney administration from the get-go, its day-to-day running made possible via the indentured labor funneled in from America's corporate-prison population.

But the guise that Melly had thought would protect her—the dashing reporter breaking a legitimately newsworthy item—only proved sustainable for a week or two after her first bombshell exclusive on the Palestinian camps. With no massive foreign tragedies or domestic police clashes to distract the news cycle, all the cable-television and elite streaming-broadcast platforms had booked her. But the moment a self-proclaimed American militia had FedExed secession papers to the media (along with a raft of credit-card statements showing an unbelievable amount of cumulative debt), the press was on to the next showdown, Citizen vs. Government of Citicard.

The retreat-into-the-brush revolutionaries of the militia, formally powerless to disgorge their student-loan and mortgage debts via the more or less shuttered organ of bankruptcy—and unlikely candidates for the future debtors' prisons—made for great television, precisely because they tended not to be traditionally photogenic.

After years of War on Terror cable exoticism, in which scenes of Middle Eastern back-alley warfare had been beamed into the American mind via the pixelated realness of green-tinted night-vision lenses, here at last was a violence of home-grown grit. Because they were evading the law, the Credit Card Burners (as they took to calling themselves, swiping and adapting a phrase from the Vietnam days) relied on spotty freeware technology to communicate with the moving-image media: old MacBooks running outdated legacy versions of Skype, Wi-Fi signals obtained in corporate-sponsored parks and the last remaining public libraries. This was broadly in keeping with the new century's cable-news aesthetic, dominated by combat-ready "embed" reporters who spoke to the viewing public (American citizens with flat-screens that captured 1080p signals in purest High Definition). Financially solvent audiences ate it up; a few of the Burners could even claim folk-hero status in certain circles, such as the hipper, under-50 private-club coterie that still idolized the *New York Times* editorial board.

But all this hadn't exactly worked out well for Melly's story. Talking about the U.S. Palestinian Internment Authority (USPIA), a bureaucracy that existed mostly as rumor when Melly broke the story in the fall of 2014, was the definition of boring TV. And the subsequent bipartisan support in Congress for her prosecution under state-secret statutes robbed her case of the only conceivable attribute—controversy—that might have kept her name in the headlines.

And so Melly was sent to work in the same camps she had exposed. Melly had ignored the hushed-tone, not-in-so-many-words warnings from the corporate lawyers while reporting the story. Though they had all sworn up and down that even talking about potential jail time was a tragedy of truly First Amendment scale, the men and women of the publication's law firm had been professionally obligated to instruct her to clam up. But this she did not do. It wasn't strictly about the deep-down values of the pose she was striking (and simultaneously narrating for the public). She wanted a shake-up in her life. And like many a white-collar criminal, she thought that testing the borders of law-abiding behavior might bring the side benefits of a new perspective—one otherwise unavailable from the list of meditation programs hosted at YogaFlow-on-Dupont.

She had overcorrected, Melly knew now—even if the major life lesson suggested by her past dozen months in the belly of the American beast had not yet been properly absorbed by her subconscious. For what was she doing, jailbreaking a Palestinian teenage boy? Fearing the violence of the prison's work-program, she had once again taken an elaborate and dangerous way out.

There was no way to rationalize her way out of feeling unbalanced, Melly thought. But after a mere quarter hour in the resort, the ex-reporter began to feel that she—and the boy too—could not stay here, in a palace of relaxation. It was *too* nice. They'd be seen by the sort of person likely to recognize her—and the sort of person with the juice to forward the intel to an interested party. At minimum, it wasn't good that Warden Lovegren had their room numbers. All he had to do, per their back-channel arrangement, was send a minion to knock at her door. It was too easy for him, and too unpredictable for Melly.

She found Ghassan. He was nearly motionless atop a queen-size mattress inside the small suite of rooms adjoining her own bungalow. "This is in-cred-ible," he said without taking his eyes off the scrolling menu of streaming-media options, imprinted with impossible crispness on a 46" screen. His deadness of affect Melly took to be a sideways suggestion that he was not meant to be bothered just now. But Melly felt strongly enough about the wisest course of action that she decided to barge ahead anyway.

"You're gonna kill me—"

"Because Palestinians are so violent, right? Wait, should I go get my blasting caps?"

"Snarling sarcasm aside, I think—rather, I know—it's best that we hightail it out of here."

The adolescent head slowly swiveled away from the screen. Its pupils were engorging with disbelief.

"Unless, of course, you'd prefer to be scooped up by some local-government potentate looking to make a name for him- or herself with the anti-immigrant crowd."

"Let 'em take me back, if that's what happens," Ghassan said, turning again to the screen. "At least I'll have however long I have as an American, with a fully stocked portfolio of entertainments." The defiant note was cut with a sad humor. Melly softened, realizing that his protest would not last forever. She wouldn't have to stomp her feet or over-make the case. He just wanted a little longer in the room, was all.

"Leaving aside, of course, the fact that the transport back to Warden Lovegren's pad might make for even worse company than yours truly," Melly offered. She hoped Ghassan heard the sympathy in her voice.

"I'm going to require a little something in the way of explanation," Ghassan said with an impressively maintained evenness as, only a few minutes later, they were scooting past the perimeter of the bungalowplex. "Or is the fact that you didn't check us out officially some sort of indication that I might lobby you into turning the car around again?"

"Yeah, probably not," she said. "Though as long as we're leaving a trail, I'd like it to not be a totally clear one."

Ghassan's face swiveled into a contemplative grimace. "So we're being followed, then?"

"I wouldn't necessarily want to denigrate Warden Lovegren's character. But whether he knows it or not, his shop might not be the most leakproof vessel in the government-contractor fleet. Also: that paradise was too close to Camp Echo; I think we'll do better with another few dozen miles between us and our former lodgings."

Ghassan seemed to accept this. "You know," he said, after a blip of mutual silence, "I only ever heard rumors about the American-prisoner layout in New Gaza. It true your set lived high on the metaphoric hog, like back at the palace we just scrambled away from? Big screens and saunas for 'physical therapy' and whatnot?"

"Nothing better to wonder about than that?"

"Hey," Ghassan said with a flash of indignance—maybe the first Melly had heard from him, which surprised and impressed her now that it had occurred. "You try being scooped up by the imperialist lackeys and repatriated into a foreign jail. You'll be amazed, the things you might wonder about, happening in realms where you're not welcome to set footstep numero uno."

"OK, OK, mea culpa," Melly backtracked, making a show of squinting at the road—as though her status as the driver might exculpate any thoughtless turns made along the simultaneous path of conversation. "But, more importantly, to your question: it wasn't any great shakes, your average accommodation for the ex-civilian prisoner-contractor."

"Yeah, I always thought that rang weird," Ghassan said, in a less aggrieved register of voice.

"From what I saw of your lodgings—which wasn't a great deal—we had it a bit better than your lot. But nothing like the spread back there, where Lovegren was hoping to keep us under administrative eye."

"Not that I have any great abiding faith in the motives of Americans, but why don't we want Lovegren keeping tabs? Kind of a 'devil you know' idea? If we get in trouble out here, we're on our own, yes?"

Melly swallowed hard. "Think of it this way: if—unbeknownst to us, even—we caused trouble out here for New Gaza's administration, the warden would not hesitate to trade us to another player in the federal bureaucracy, no questions asked. My bedroom at Camp Echo was nicer than yours, sure, but both of us have about the same amount of negotiating power."

"More or less zero."

"Correct. I'm sort of counting on Warden Lovegren having a panicky shit-fit once he realizes you're not nodding off in front of an HBO GO account. We get in trouble, we reach out to him; if he wants us back, we call in the cavalry to help us out—and maybe score ourselves some better terms."

"Such as?"

"Well, I don't want to get your hopes up too high," Melly started. "But there are rumors of...Palestinian 'notables,' in some of the bigger cities, who are less formally 'encamped.' Not citizens, by any means, but a life of less-bleak internment. Enjoyable, even, I've heard." Melly did not want to give too much voice to rumors she wasn't sure she could substantiate. But she owed the kid at least a little in the way of hope.

"Yeah, I know," Ghassan said. "The Stateless Elect, is what they're called."

The reporter lobe in Melly's brain started sending off alarm signals at a volume that she found excruciating. At minimum, the rumors—mostly whispered among national-security beat reporters and otherwise-uninformed conspiracy jackasses—might be true. They were at least alive enough to find purchase in Palestinian culture post–Nakba 2.0.

Instinctively, Melly wanted to file a note to her editor. It took a moment to realize that she had no editor. She had an 18-year-old Palestinian man-child, and that was it. But as it turned out, he had something of an editor's mind—the ability to see the weakness in a developing story, and check Melly's train of thought. He asked, "How do you know this car isn't actually being tracked? GPS or whatever? We have to get rid of it, right?" Melly almost smacked an open palm against her forehead, but refrained in the interests of seeming like an adult not given to excessive doubt or self-recrimination.

He was right: they'd need to ditch the Lexus. If she'd been smarter, Melly thought as she drove, she'd have asked the warden for a map with at least rough indicators marking the other known Palestinian zones. And maybe a shittier, less noticeable ride. But the plan had come together so quickly: only a few hours had elapsed between her formal proposal and Warden Lovegren putting it into action. As it was, both she and Ghassan were flying blind, in an area of Wyoming where citizens might be of greater or lesser inclination to view someone like Ghassan as an escapee. Sure, she'd ditched her U.S. Department of Corrections–issued orange wardrobe, and she looked official enough in her simple wool suit. (It was cut for a man—the warden's deputy had swiped it from a hanger in the closet of an office across the hall from his own—and Melly was rocking it with a slightly asymmetrical, louche quality.) But Ghassan would still carry his Mediterranean complexion anywhere they went, despite his own change of clothes (into an over-large sweatshirt and jeans). "We're going to find a garage and negotiate an on-site trade," Melly announced, as though this had been her plan all along. "That way we'll score some cash, while covering our tracks."

"How will we keep moving, though, if we're trading in our wheels for cash?" Ghassan asked.

"For cash and a much shittier set of wheels, I meant."

"Some people just don't know how to live with nice things," the boy said with a light-touch mournfulness that Melly found funny. He really was a comedian.

How did she look to him, though? Melly couldn't tell if he bought her current mood of composed cool. She kept glancing over, searching Ghassan's face for signs of annoyance or unsteadiness. If he ceased to trust her, he might just strike out on his own.

"Also," he said, "isn't this car, like, very obviously not ours to sell? Government plates and our not having the registration and all that good stuff?"

"Well," Melly said, "it's just a matter of finding the right buyer. The official look of this beast has got to be of use to some in-the-bush citizens' outfit."

"Great. So we're going to give some nativist shit-kickers a vehicular disguise."

Melly almost shot back that the necessity of ditching the car had been Ghassan's own contribution to the conversation, but remembered that she was pretending to have thought of that already. So instead she rode in silence and hoped the young man would not continue to press the issue.

"That garage no good for any reason?" Ghassan asked with a teen's affected laziness of drawl. Without saying "Oh, shit" or "Sorry, my head was in another place," Melly stabbed at the brakes, rolled the vehicle backward a couple dozen yards, and hung a right toward the dimly visible strip mall whose exit sign included prominent Tire Chief signage—a capital T joined to a C in a cartoonishly exaggerated font. In the distance, a three-dimensional rendering of the same logo appeared high in the sky, like an advertisement for a fast-food oasis in some automotive desert.

Inside the garage, Melly soon realized she had no experience haggling over the sale of a used item. Certainly not a Lexus bearing government plates. The supervising attendant—a tall, bespectacled man in his late fifties, clad in overalls and a gimme cap that only mostly covered his thinning, gray curl-tufts of hair—seemed to know this, and enjoyed his situational advantage.

He spoke to Melly as though she had made the offer in some foreign language. "You want to what?" he said, cupping a hand to his ear. It was a cruel and blunt way of making her repeat the awkward offer. Melly was also aware that she was failing in front of Ghassan, who was hanging back by the rear bumper.

"I'd...like...to see...if there's any interest, maybe on behalf of your boss..."

"GRIFT!" the garage attendant yelled. Melly thought he was accusing her of running a scam. But a shorter, younger man appeared, answering to the word as if it were a name. He had been working on a tractor deeper in the garage's recesses.

"Hey, Grift," the first attendant said. "This grande dame here says she wants to trade in this number, for another car and a little cash. Now, I'm not a lawyer or anything, but what do you think of that?"

"It's entrapment, if you're the law," Grift told her.

"I'm not the law," she said.

"Oh, she has to say that," Grift said to the first attendant.

Ghassan stepped forward. "If she was the law, would she be trying to sell you a car with the government plates still on it?"

Both employees smirked at the kid, and Melly immediately wished that he had not spoken up. Though he certainly was a dear for trying.

The taller attendant walked up to Ghassan. "The law could do that. Try some reverse-double-fake-out action." Ghassan's lower lip was quivering, and Melly moved to step between them. As she did, she heard another voice call out from the rear of the building.

"Jerry, who you terrorizin' now?"

The voice belonged to another tall man, in another work shirt streaked with grease. But this one had a friendlier face—even if the skin under both cheekbones carried a fair amount of acne scarring. His unwashed blond hair seemed stylishly unkempt instead of indifferently handled. Melly hoped this man was superior to the first attendant in this organization.

"Woman come in, trying to sell us stolen government property," the first attendant told his blond colleague.

"Says she's not the law," Grift added.

"Is that true?" the blond gentleman asked Melly.

She was being given a chance to try this again. Thankfully, during the back and forth between the garage employees, she'd had time to concoct the halfway decent lie she should have driven in with.

"Sorry, boys," she said. "Clearly you can see I'm not used to this type of thing." She looked at the first attendant. "And I owe you a slight apology, for not explaining myself very well. And to you too, Grift."

Grift smiled, as though happy she'd addressed him by his nickname.

"The truth is, I am a little bit connected to the administration of the nation's legal system." She held her hands up, as if forestalling objections. "I'm not a prosecutor; I don't arrest anyone—that's not why I'm here." Melly pointed at Ghassan, who looked shocked to have attention foisted back in his direction. "This poor child's family just suffered a...tragic loss, over in New Gaza," Melly said, meeting the blond man's eyes. "I'm a social worker, and it's my job to get him to the nearest camp where he has family relations."

She looked at the three men; they were hooked. Waving one hand back in the direction of the open Wyoming highway, she proceeded. "Now, I'm sure you boys keep up with the news—and so you've probably read, or heard a little talk, regarding the blasts in the nearby New Gaza camp last night."

"Just what little they see fit to tell us regular citizens," the elder attendant said with a trace of spite.

"It's just terr'ble," the blond man added with a real attempt at sympathy. "Are those explosions what account for your ferrying of this here trembling child?"

Melly looked at Ghassan. She wouldn't call him trembling, exactly—but the boy was clearly shaken. "In all honestly, gents," Melly said, "between you and me: I'm afraid to be traveling these streets with government plates. Which is why I came through here, looking for a trade."

The blond man looked at Melly, then at Ghassan. "It's a shame that some folks do act out violently toward the camp authorities 'round these parts. I can understand what you mean, thinking you'd be vulnerable riding around in this tax-dollar-bought Lexus."

"Rorty, are you buyin' this?" the elder attendant asked. The blond man patted him on the shoulder in a way that confirmed, for Melly, that he was the boss.

"'Course ah do. And it's our civic duty to help out, when called upon." He spoke with a drawl that Melly assumed was at least partway affected.

"That's very lovely of you, Rorty," she said. "And rest assured, I don't need any favorable terms of sale here. You just tell me what's available, in terms of slightly less conspicuous models, and then how much cash on top will make the deal square."

The man they called Grift melted away. The elder attendant looked sickened; he stormed off when Rorty brought out an early-aughts Honda and counted out just shy of five thousand dollars in cash for Melly to take with her.

"It's easier if we just shake on this," Melly told Rorty as they prepared to leave. "But if you'd like me to have some paperwork sent over later, that I could certainly do."

"You do whatever's best for the government," Rorty replied. "And for this here dear child."

CHAPTER ELEVEN:

NEWSPOWMEOW STUDIOS,
ENGLEWOOD CLIFFS, NEW JERSEY
THURSDAY, AUGUST 6, 2015, 11:00 A.M. (EASTERN TIME)

Three hours had elapsed since Crissy had left the intern at her two-bedroom pad in the West Village. The sporting thing might have been to leave him a note—something like, *Thanks for the endorphin buffet, dude. Feel free to carb up in my fridge. Or bounce if you feel like it. In any case, I'll be back when I'm back. Do as you will!*

Instead, almost immediately after locking the apartment building's security door behind her—and then bounding into the town car that had been waiting half a block up the street—Crissy had all but forgotten him. She was thinking exclusively about the fact that her father had sent Persia VanSlyke to investigate the rumor that a potential Democratic U.S. Senate candidate had once conceived a child out of wedlock. And that her dear old pop had thought there was some underreported string in the story of last night's New Gaza explosion. How could they be connected?

Once past NewsPowMeow's front-desk security turnstiles, she had started prepping for her first evening broadcast. Normally there were emails of collated links from at least two "anchor producers," plus "to read" printed material clipped together and organized into a stack on her desk.

But her inbox and desktop were bare of underling attention. At noon, while clicking through the top national news websites on her own, Crissy received a suspenseful, terse email from the vice president of programming, requesting her presence at a 1:30 meeting. Standards and Legal had been cc'd.

If she had to face down representatives from those departments, she'd prefer to do it carrying a big stack of important-looking papers. That was how most anchors were supposed to travel from one point on the studio floor to another—as though they were bookish college seniors, weighed down with information that would be synthesized in the next segment, after a commercial break.

The paper shuffle was a touch more complex for the women anchors, who—at least at this network—were made to stand for most of a given hour. Otherwise known as "first position," this is where Crissy would invariably remain, ramrod-upright, during the majority of her broadcast time, shoulders pinned back, blissfully unobstructed by the big oaky desks that came standard for male anchors. Crissy's only companion in these hours—save for the producers piped in via IFB earbud, and the red light above whichever camera was live—was a lithe little table, ass-height, on which she could place her prep papers.

She knew this, had made peace with "it" before it was even formalized as part of her employment—and so on most days could behave as though she were fine with that state of play. Like an overdetermined yogi expounding on the long-term benefits of her practice while struggling to achieve a terrifically difficult pose, Crissy liked to say that she fully owned her imprisonment within sexist constraints, that she was subtly subverting them from her position.

In select, female-dominated company, Crissy might talk with fantastic (and subtly self-recriminatory) panache about someday taking the money and running off to start her own news organization. The Coven of the Formerly Masturbated-To Hotties Evening News Hour. Her first guests would be the unacknowledged harem of some Gulf-area potentate, and they would talk productively about the ways in which women are invited to trade upon their looks, in all cultures. Crissy's fantasies along such lines became more energetically detailed and strange-sounding right after she had to suffer through a punishingly dull meeting. She suspected that she would be enduring one this afternoon, before her evening broadcast.

After being welcomed into the 20th-floor inner sanctum by Programming VP Clyde Huntsman—a tall, avuncular man with two-and-a-half chins and only a few more wisps of hair—Crissy saw that her phalanx of managers, agents and attorneys had arrived before her, all present and accounted for.

"What the actual fuck," Crissy whispered to her television agent, a ruthless, sixty-something woman with whom Crissy felt no bond. In fact, the anchor was fairly sure the agent did not respect her at all—an intuition that seemed confirmed when, instead of responding, the woman silently joined the row of paid individuals who made up "Team Crissy." Seated on one side of a near-black wood slab of a table, their gaze was fixed on the row of NewsPowMeow executives on the other side. All of the station execs, in turn, had their eyes fixed upon Crissy. These paper pushers had the satisfied look of people who knew their jobs would never be in jeopardy. Behind them, the unimpressively desolate northern New Jersey skyline sat with nowhere else to go.

"Christine!" VP Clyde barked enthusiastically. He had called Crissy by her proper, full name, she suspected, as a way of distancing himself from the culture-coarsening on-screen persona they had all created for her in collaboration. As if to say: *yes, nasty business, all that remorseless sexualizing that we need and profit from—for reasons necessary and proper, of course—but here in the corporate office, we need have none of it! Heavens, no! Scotch?*

Except no one was offering her Scotch.

"Clyde," Crissy responded as she let the man take her hand. "Or should I say Mr. Huntsman?" VP Clyde winced and smiled and shook hands at once—*oh no, please let's not stand on ceremony*—as though Crissy's needless formality had actually been wounding. "It's just that, when I see so many decked-out fancies here in Englewood Cliffs," Crissy explained to the room, "all on account of li'l ol' me—I start to get nervous."

"No need for nervousness!" Clyde boomed. "All will be taken care of, don't you worry. Last thing we need before your evening broadcast, nervousness." The heavyset VP had rotated around to the head of the conference table and allowed himself a slight, effortful exhale as he dropped into the seat's cream-colored, no doubt expensive leather cushion. "Though there are some things we need to...confirm."

After taking her own place between an even number of lawyers and handlers on each side, Crissy was handed a portfolio of documents. First up was the employment application of the intern she had fucked last night. Apparently, the young man (whose name turned out to be Eric) had received his undergraduate degree from West Point (and here's where his musculature started to make more sense), had served in Afghanistan, been stationed as a reserve out of Nebraska for a couple years, and was now in his second year of grad school, in Columbia's journalism program. Crissy turned to another page in the briefing, which she immediately understood to be more relevant to the meeting.

This paperwork Crissy recognized. It was the indemnifying waiver that any NewsPowMeow underling had to fill out before acceding to a "romantic" advance from a senior employee of the company. Crissy had reviewed the same paperwork, marked with Eric's sign-offs, in her town car before commanding him to go down on her.

"Do you recognize this bit of business?" VP Clyde asked Crissy.

"Sure—it's…," she began, wanting to say the intern's name— *Eric*—though it got caught in her mouth, unfamiliar as it was. "The intern filled this out before we spent our first—and should I add only?—night together."

"He gave it to you directly? It passed from his hand to yours?" VP Clyde had shorn nearly all of the cornball bonhomie from his affect; he was lawyerly now in his questioning—almost excessively so—while one of his assistants took notes on a tablet in the rear corner of the room.

"Ah—no, I don't believe so," Crissy said to VP Clyde's evident, scowling displeasure. "To be clear: it was in the sheaf of papers that had been laid on my desk before the D block in my last hour. It was filed underneath the scripts. The intern—E-Eric—he

135

was my anchor producer last night. Given my prior invitation, I took the positioning of the paperwork to be, like, er—well, an erotic gesture. As though he was showing me how everything was in order, and that by returning the paperwork in a manner so similar to his working-hours duty, he intended to keep serving and preparing me for the rest of the night."

Crissy looked at her agent. It occurred to her that this woman probably knew better than to fuck an intern. But Crissy was relieved to discover that all of the professionals in the room, save perhaps VP Clyde, were unfazed by Crissy's personal disclosure and ensuing embarrassment.

"Unfortunate turn, this one," said VP Clyde, before remembering that, per his corporate behavioral preference, any articulation of bad news ought to conclude with a sunny-side-up exclamation point. "I mean, for our side, it's not ideal!"

"But I thought the point of the waiver was so that we were in the clear," Crissy said. "That I could go to town with him, et cetera."

"Oh, absolutely! That is its purpose, more or less," said VP Clyde. "But then there is the matter of the last page. You will note that on the following page—its upper third is reserved for signatures—is blank. Neither Eric nor you insisted on the full execution of the document."

Crissy flipped to the page she had not known to look for. It was as blank as VP Clyde's forced good humor. "Hm, okay—so that's not good, I guess?" Crissy said to the room, hoping that she would be at least partially contradicted by someone telling her things would be set right, and quickly. No one stepped up to inform her that this was fine—that it was a mistake anyone might have made—and the anchor realized that some more self-flagellation would be expected. "I don't know how I could have missed that."

"Well, don't get too down on yourself," VP Clyde said. "Really, it's the least of our worries at the moment. Or, rather, it's an adjacent worry."

"Is the guy...dead or something? I mean, God, why are we really here?" Crissy asked. Her agent patted her arm without conviction, while Clyde let out an aggrieved hoot.

"If only things were so clear-cut and final," VP Clyde replied, shaking his head, before quickly adding, "I'm sorry, is that too dark?"

Crissy's middle-aged lawyer, perched two seats to her right, on the other side of her agent, cleared his throat nervously; when no one objected to his claiming the floor, he turned to his client and flashed a laser-whitened smile. "It's been suggested that your intern, or rather the student in question—subordinate, really, if we're speaking technically—by which of course I mean this Eric, has represented himself incompletely.... "

A short woman with stylishly clumpy bangs and horn-rim glasses, sitting to VP Clyde's left, interrupted Crissy's lawyer: "Jesus, man, spit it out." When her command was not heeded, she addressed Crissy: "We think he's NSA."

"What?" the anchor asked.

"Or CIA or something—who the hell can keep track anymore," the VP's deputy said. "Anyway, intern-based cover stories are sort of the intel world's new covert thing, when it comes to surveilling media figures. Something we've only tripped over recently."

"And we haven't reported on it why?"

"New frontier, in terms of liability!" VP Clyde said, as if extolling the virtues of a new stain remover.

"We've been waved off of it by the White House," the deputy added. "It's part of a new-ish program of theirs—and until today, we haven't had anything resembling hard evidence."

"How does today enter into it?" Crissy asked.

"In wanting to see how big a pile of shit we were in, with regard to you having sex with a grad-student intern absent a fully executed situational waiver, we called up to Columbia and realized...this guy is not a student. Never even enrolled."

Crissy leafed once more through the portfolio she'd been handed. Included were letters of recommendation on Columbia letterhead (signed, in one instance, by a professor whose name Crissy knew to be real) and a current-looking Columbia transcript. "So these documents—"

"Fake," the deputy said.

"Damn good forgeries, though!" VP Clyde said, sounding like a guy on a late-'90s I Can't Believe It's Not Butter ad.

"But this is great? That we have the government cold. Let's put it in tonight's A block, yeah?"

"Only if you want to leave yourself open to a tabloidy exposé about your sex life with interns," the deputy said. "You can bet you were videotaped, or audio recorded, at a minimum."

"But he's not an intern!"

The deputy scanned the row of Crissy's professional hangers-on. "Any of them can tell you—as can, really, anyone who's taken time to read the company policy—that this corporate-indemnification form, the very same one that was explained to you

138

in your employee training two years ago, does not merely cover interns."

"It covers government agents engaged in press intimidation and domestic surveillance?"

Crissy's agent turned to her client, speaking for the first time and touching her arm more forcefully. "Officially? No," she said.

Crissy was shocked to find the woman's hand resting on her right arm. It might have looked, to others in the room, like a soothing gesture—but Crissy took it as a shackling force. "Unofficially," the agent continued, "your failure to keep yourself and the company 100 percent free of vulnerability on this score serves as a de facto yapping opportunity for those whose mouths we'd otherwise be able to force shut."

"I see," Crissy said. *Exactly how much shit am I going to have to eat over this?*, she wondered. Trying to reassert control over the conversation—she was a journalist; it was time to start defining the issue instead of playing catch-up to what had already been discussed in some other room—Crissy added a newly skeptical tone to her next question. "So the corporation's remedy here is what? Firing me? What's the damage?"

VP Clyde's deputy seemed to have assumed control as NewsPowMeow's mouthpiece. "The company's concern is the amount of reputational damage this intern might be able to inflict on one of the company's assets. By which, of course, I mean you."

Crissy winced. Even VP Clyde seemed to register the aggressively possessive quality to his underling's phrasing. "We're concerned for you, is all!" he said.

"That's all?" Crissy asked. "Doesn't sound it."

"Ho! Let's take the temperature down, then," he said. He patted the corner of his deputy's legal pad, which was resting on the conference table. In another era, Crissy thought, he might have grazed or grabbed at the woman's knee or shoulder. And though she was still angry with her unexpected antagonist in this meeting, Crissy was glad to see that the corporate paterfamilias knew better than to touch a subordinate female employee while also telling her to calm down. Even if it was because he had become judiciously lawsuit-aware—in the precise way that Crissy had proven not to be, in the case of intern-agent Eric—she elected to judge it, in real time, as gender-and-workplace progress of an acceptable and even enviable strain.

"For now, we're dismissing Eric the intern," the deputy said.

"Absolutely!" VP Clyde added.

"And, in consultation with your team," the deputy continued, "we're going to suspend you for a week. Just as a show of good faith that we took this issue seriously. And that you paid some nominal price. We've also called you to this meeting to underline the reasons for following the corporate guidelines to the letter. Think of it as a useful review, in the event that you commence any future activities along similar lines. I know it's not sexy, but these signatures are of utmost importance."

Crissy was astonished by the aggression in the woman's word choice. "Sexy," uttered in a corporate meeting like this one, was never used in connection with acts of coitus; it was employed to describe a slightly more zippy approach to the on-air graphics or the increased attractiveness of a financial-incentives package. Was VP Clyde's deputy actually having fun at Crissy's expense?

Messing with her by restyling the argot of corporate-speak with the erotic cloak of which it had previously been denuded?

"Noted," Crissy said to the assembled group. "Are we done?"

"Yes!" VP Clyde boomed.

As the assembled corporate shills gathered their papers in preparation for whatever knives-out meeting they would be attending next, Crissy felt a desire to rub all their faces in the grubbiness of the network's business. "Who's going to tell my bestest private-video buddies that for the next week they'll have to jack off to something else before bedtime?" asked the star of NewsPowMeow's 9 p.m. and midnight broadcasts. Everyone acted as though they hadn't heard her.

Beyond the elevator bay, past the semicircular check-in area —which was staffed by no fewer than two receptionists at all times —the company had installed a ballooning, expansive employee lounge with floor-to-ceiling windows. Crissy lingered near its stiff couches, one knee pressed against a leather-upholstered ottoman, and stared out the windows at the tax-friendly northern New Jersey county where NewsPowMeow was quartered. She dialed her father's number.

"Daughter," Beverly answered, "it occurs to me, now, that I owed you another call."

"You owe me more than that," she said. "You owe me information."

"I'll be owing you still, I'm afraid," he replied, to a humorless silence on the other end. "It's only that I don't have much to offer just yet."

"Start with what you do know."

Crissy heard her father sigh. "There's a new edge to your voice."

"I've been suspended, if you must know."

"Oh, dear," Beverly said. "Well, why not relax? Forget chasing stories for a few days. And when you're back, then maybe I'll have something for—"

Crissy didn't often interrupt her father. No matter how intense their conversational sparring, when they were engaged in source-and-reporter banter instead of family-time talk they extended each other the courtesy of allowing main clauses to resolve. But on this afternoon, the NewsPowMeow anchor had no interest in taking the scenic route to the main point. "Kind of hard to kick back, Pops, once you realize the government has been spying on you," she said. "Kind of makes a girl want to bolt out West for a spell."

"Like, regular spying? Phone intercepts? That's not such a surprise, is it?"

"More than that. The personal touch. HUMINT, I think, is the trade abbreviation? My very own case officer in the satellite-ops room."

"Nasty," Beverly agreed. "I've heard a bit out of school about such things in recent months. Seems it's all part of the new normal, after some of the security breaches."

Her father wasn't in the intelligence community, but he insisted on using their terminology for some reason. "By 'security breaches,' of course, you mean 'stellar public-service journalism.'"

"Oh, let's not fight on too many fronts at once, darling," Beverly said.

"I don't want any fights. Just answers. And, thing is: I'm pretty sure your asking about Wyoming the other night had something to do with my tip about Meyerbeer."

Her father didn't have a snappy retort ready.

"I'd demand to know 'true or false?' right now, except I think you just told me."

If Beverly had heard his daughter, he gave no aural indication. The only sound that reached Crissy's ear was a grunt that suggested her father was shifting the lion's share of his seated girth from an alignment that overly favored one buttock. His daughter felt a pang of guilt over not being there, in Beverly's D.C. home office, to help him navigate the ever-increasing number of obstacles thrown up by a progressively constricting range of mobility. She said nothing until Beverly broke the mutual impasse.

"Hugh Lovegren. Administrator in New Gaza. That's all I can give you now."

"Oh, that's great," Crissy cried, peck-typing the name into her Notes app and speaking simultaneously into the phone's mic.

"The lead may already be, I should say, cold."

"Seriously, that's fine; you're the best." She paused. "Say, how long has it been since you've worked out of the office?"

"I'm in my office right now."

"I mean the regular office. With the other DSCC folk? With the normal people?"

"Oh, I'm fine," Beverly said. "My absence is no great loss to the others in the D-trip or the D-S. It's better for all concerned if I just indulge my...sensibilities. My solitude as a personal style. And as long as I continue to not fuck up, I expect I'll have a job."

She had already known that her father was depressed. But hearing it like this made it all the harder to take. Whenever Beverly started talking about the solid nature of his employment, his daughter knew enough to be worried. Should she be thinking of ways to work out of D.C.? Should she move her father up to the West Village? New York seemed like a terrible place to grow old, though.

"Pops, I want to ask after your health, your state of mind—all the daddy-daughter things that really should constitute the majority of this conversation."

Beverly laughed. "Daughter, just go. Find the story, write what you learn."

"I will, Pop."

"And stay safe, yes? Gets dangerous in the West."

"I'm lining up some muscle, right after we hang up."

"Good. And come see me sometime, eh? After you catch up with Persia."

That night, as the NewsPowMeow company town car rolled up next to her building, Crissy leaned forward—almost vaulting into Larry the driver's lap—after the headlights revealed an individual sitting in wait upon her stoop. She was mad at her troublesome spy-slash-intern for all the obvious reasons, but was also glad to see him again—and not just because she intended to bully him into accompanying her on the imminent flight to Wyoming. In the spectral and faintly kaleidoscopic white heat of the car's brights, Eric gave a half-hearted wave that doubled as a shield for his eyes.

"Wouldn't you know it," he spoke-yelled as she dragged her bag out of the car and smiled goodbye at Larry. "I lost my internship today." God, he thought he was awfully cute, didn't he?

Problem was he wasn't wrong. She walked halfway up the stoop and sat on the stair just above Eric's large shoulders. "Well, that's the worst fucking news I've heard all day," she said, leaning forward to mess up a lock of his short hair. The town car had withdrawn into the renewing darkness. "Oh wait, that's not correct. I've heard stories today that would make a lowly intern's already-tousled hair twist about even more cylindrically."

"You know you start to talk funny when you get turned on?"

"Who says I'm turned on?"

"OK, why don't we go inside and see?"

She playfully slapped at his face. "How about you come with me to the airport?"

"What'll I tell my real job?"

"Whatever I wind up doing, obviously. Same as before. I'd like to think we've entered the remorselessly transparent portion of our dalliance."

CHAPTER TWELVE:

CAMP ECHO WARDEN'S CHAMBERS,
GAZA, WYOMING
THURSDAY, AUGUST 6, 2015, 9:00 P.M. (MOUNTAIN TIME)

Warden Lovegren had predicted that a Democratic operative from D.C. would assail his sanctum before the week was out. But he had not expected it to be the same one he'd booted out this very morning. And he hadn't expected the operative to look like—well, he wouldn't like to speculate, now, would he?

He remembered a panel, some nine months back, conducted by a D.C. functionary from the Coordinated Response Apparatus for Palestinian Settlements. It was back in the organization's earliest days, last fall. The event in question was led by a small, well-coiffed woman whose job, apparently, was to shuttle from one privately contracted camp to the next and educate dinosaurs like old Lovegren about the needs of any employees who might, at some point or another, announce themselves as "gender nonconforming." The warden had fallen asleep and snored during the presentation.

Upon being told afterward, he had at first been embarrassed. But once he discovered that his fellow administrators had absorbed his somnolence as a well-earned, not-so-subtle rebuke, he quickly expanded upon what had begun as an unintended insult.

After the break, he made quite a show of tossing some paper handouts into the nearest trashcan. The papers had been ensconced in an off-white folder whose fancy embossed texture had presumably been intended to approximate richly detailed leatherwork, but which looked cheap and doomed to aesthetic failure. Lovegren got another laugh for binning the materials.

Now, with this Democratic operative seated in front of his desk, the warden realized he hadn't bothered to give a second's thought to the transgender community. He had seen it discussed more and more on cable television programs, of course, and thus was just as educated as any other minimally aware consumer of news. And he knew there was, in general, an increased public understanding of those who did not find themselves satisfied with what was called the "outdated gender binary." But he hadn't thought about the actual people involved in all this. Not since the orientation he'd mostly slept through.

"Your last name is VanSlyke," Lovegren began, with a stalling lameness he hoped to put across as lack of concern.

"Yes," the operative allowed. "Persia is my first name."

Persia sounded awfully feminine. But still, he decided not to chance it with a "Ms."

"Forgive me," Lovegren replied. "My deputy here"— Lovegren gave a look in the direction of Mr. Clamp, who had stationed himself at the office's long wall, equidistant from the door and the far corner—"merely said you were from the Democratic Senatorial Campaign Committee. An 'operative' we sadly had to rush out of here, early this morning, due to the unfortunate security concerns. In any event, my deputy neglected to pass on your precise title."

The operative sat still, as though unaware that Lovegren had asked a question. VanSlyke's assuredly male companion swiveled his head around to get the measure of the warden's deputy.

"Would you...perhaps...have a card?" the warden pressed.

"I'm the director of counter-opposition research," Persia said. *Aha!* Lovegren thought; now he could address this person as "Director VanSlyke," obviating the need for a gendered pronoun. He was proud of his caution.

"Meaning you investigate potential candidates before the other team can square off against them?"

Director VanSlyke nodded. "Among other things."

Allowing himself a chuckle, Lovegren asked, "Anyone in these environs announced for 2016?"

Had Persia emitted a small but exasperated sigh in response? Lovegren thought he saw a crack in the otherwise calm demeanor, just before the operative said, "There's no need for us to go back and forth for dozens upon dozens of delightfully coy rounds. I'm here to look for a child. Ghassan Khouri. Is he in your care?"

"Director VanSlyke, listen here, your boss wouldn't be"— Lovegren pretended not to have the name readily at his tongue—"a certain...pardon, I do have a lot of names to keep track of...ah yes, Mr. Beverly Steindler, perhaps? Had an altogether odd chat with the fellow on the phone just before the violence commenced last night. He identified himself as a DSCC man, and now you're here." Lovegren glanced at VanSlyke's plus-one, who had made no move toward an introduction. "And you've brought along a rather taciturn companion, as well."

The companion directed a brief look toward VanSlyke, as though asking permission to speak. Receiving no intelligible guidance either way, he pressed his lips together, then opened with, "My name is Chilton Mey—"

VanSlyke's left palm suddenly rose no more than two inches from the chair's armrest and formed a stop sign—a casual variant on the universally understood signal for *shut the fuck up*. Chilton halted, mid-surname, and diverted his gaze to the floor.

"He's my intern. And his biography is not relevant to this discussion," VanSlyke said.

Under different circumstances, Warden Lovegren might have called out Director VanSlyke on such an evident falsehood. But right this second he also needed to not look pale or concerned. For he had already heard enough to know that the man with VanSlyke was a Meyerbeer.

Very troubling. It might have sent a lesser warden into convulsions. But the Lovegren ego was gratified, since its owner's instincts had held that Melly Shroud knew what she was talking about (even if she had her own reasons to seek liberation, and seemed unstable to boot). Now she had been proven correct in the main—Dennett Meyerbeer really was running for the U.S. Senate. Which meant that Lovegren had acted correctly. A part of him had hoped that he had simply been fooled by an insane but persuasive ex-journalist. In that case, he could have mounted a search party and recaptured both inmates, quickly and quietly. It would have made for a restoration of order—and perhaps some better sleep. Now, instead, he was on the cusp of a longer, harder-to-navigate game of hide-and-seek.

"Now will you answer me?" VanSlyke asked.

"Pardon?"

"A Palestinian orphan, name of Ghassan Khouri. Approximately 18 years of age. Ring a bell?"

Warden Lovegren adopted an expansiveness of tone that he hoped would be sufficient to divert the course of the conversation. "Director VanSlyke, please understand! I'm sure there is someone who answers to Ghassan Khouri in Camp Echo. Probably more than one individual so named."

Persia found the warden's attempts to wriggle out from under the question unbearable—but pushed hir annoyance underneath a veneer of cold efficiency. "Can it be very difficult for you to search a database and control for age, then? To whittle down the results?"

VanSlyke would not be put off, the warden finally understood. He would have to stall for time in a less friendly manner. "Much as we all seek to accommodate political elites around here," Lovegren began, "I'm afraid it's just not the done thing to release, willy-nilly, the locations of Palestinian residents to political sources—which is to say, strictly, nongovernmental ones."

Director VanSlyke's eyes narrowed.

"Don't despair," Lovegren added, hoping to save some vestige of companionability. "There's a process for you to apply for that information. A bit over-involved with the proverbial red tape, between the two of us, your friend, and my deputy, mind. It's only that I'm afraid I have to insist on the protocol."

After the group had left his office (VanSlyke's man without communicating anything at all, save for a desultory good-bye wave), the warden sent an email to his deputy. Clamp had probably read all of the government manuals on transgender sensitivity—if only as a means to best the other young white men in comprehending bureaucratic minutiae. It would do to use this as an advantage. All the same, Lovegren found the mercenary efficiency of his Rhodes-scholar subordinate fearsome. He knew that a time would come when Clamp would make some move against him. While the warden had been entertaining his guests, the deputy had stood at the rear of the room. At one point, when their eyes had briefly met, the deputy offered a small smirk-and-eye-roll combination, which the warden knew was meant to convey loyalty through a surreptitious dismissal of the interlopers who had trod into their mutual territory. Instead, the young man's look sent cold shivers into the nerves over Lovegren's shoulder blades, and conjured up the image of a serpent flexing its musculature and moistening the joints of its jaw.

Clamp knew about Melly Shroud and her sanctioned flight from camp, young Palestinian in tow, but Lovegren had taken care to keep the child's identity to himself. Now, thanks to the Democratic operative's questioning, the deputy had a name to connect to the face: Ghassan Khouri.

Better to give the deputy something to do, right away. In his email, Lovegren tasked him with writing up a quick primer on the latest in transgender studies. "The more academic the better," Lovegren advised. He didn't want to read it all, necessarily; he was hoping to bury his assistant under a week's worth of effort.

And perhaps he would even skim the results of the file. He really did owe it to himself to become more aware of the world outside New Gaza's walls. In his own defense, he thought, he had been busy these past few seasons; once nominated for the executive-warden position, he'd had all manner of cultural reading to catch up on.

Very little of this material had been second nature to him— the basic history of Middle Eastern social evolution, from the Ottoman era forward, was dull to read, given how obvious the rooting interest was in each case (depending on the bias inherent in each writer's perspective). And so, while preparing to take on his new contractual position with the U.S. government, he was like as not to think he had done his duty toward states of mind and culture and orientation that were not his own. Quite contrary to the government's own predictions, transgender affairs had come up barely at all during his tenure. To his knowledge, he had no employees who wrestled with such questions. At least not publicly. (But ah: was that the catch? That he could have helped those private sufferers live more publicly fulfilling lives, if only he'd run the camp in a more conscientious manner? If that was the real game, the warden thought now, he would have to admit that he'd been sitting it out entirely.)

Lovegren had heard whispers among the camp's heath-care staffers about a few residents who had questions (and sometimes demands) along the lines of access to this or that service—but it was easily handled by Lovegren's subordinate staff, and never came across his own desk. It took an effort to see beyond these blinders, and as the warden reflected on this reality later in the evening, he realized that it had taken being spooked by another male bureaucrat's potential challenge to remind him of that weakness in his character. Something to work on down the road if he managed to survive *l'affair Meyerbeer*, the warden promised himself.

CHAPTER THIRTEEN:

A WYOMING HIGHWAY
THURSDAY, AUGUST 6, 2015, 9:50 P.M. (MOUNTAIN TIME)

For the first half hour of the drive, after the gates of Camp Echo had clenched shut behind them, Persia had assumed that Chilton's testy silence was meant to punish hir for the way ze'd shut him up back in the warden's office. Many men favored this language, licking their wounds with a sharply articulated sullenness (as if blaming the world for the silent treatment they were giving it in turn), and over the years Persia had been presented with ample opportunity to reflect upon it. Ze knew that ze would never quite make emotional sense of it, let alone adopt it as a trait of hir own fluid gender expression.

The streak of male silence had continued for sufficient duration that Persia at last assumed the young Meyerbeer scion had up and fallen asleep—a less aggressive act than freezing hir out of the conversation, but still selfish, all the same. To pass the time as ze drove them deeper into the crackling, early-evening dryness of Wyoming, Persia indulged in remembering some of hir fondest past conversations. Ze wasn't often given to sentimental reflection—but this was shaping up to be a duller evening than ze'd anticipated.

Taking that first step around the corner abutting memory lane could be a touch depressing, especially given that the "girl talk" ze had shared with college-era dorm-mates had been some of the best ze was likely ever to have. This was unfortunate not just because those discussions dated from a period when Persia had been actively suppressing hir intuition regarding hir assigned-at-birth gender, but because "girl talk" was now no longer an option, strictly speaking. Cisgender women could talk a good game about being trans inclusive, and being open to a penumbra of sisterhoods, but that wasn't how it shook out in the subtlest, most crucial byways of community building. Ze had not managed to keep up with any of hir erstwhile fellow ladies from Wesleyan.

Yes, there were tendrils of social-media connectivity between them still; one member of the old group had even interviewed Persia in recent years, during the brief period when ze was experimenting with the more strictly transmasculine name "Percy." Specifically, they'd talked about Percy's encounters with transphobia for an article that eventually found its way into a queer-studies anthology. Percy's interviewer—one among the great number of women named Emily in the East Coast academic corridor—had, during their mutual years at Wesleyan, spent some time as a size-acceptance activist, though she was only very slightly overweight (and even then only by egregiously unforgiving New York City–adjacent cultural norms).

Reading Emily's article upon publication—it had taken so long to come into print that ze was back to using "Persia" with all audiences—ze had felt an alarming, hollow feeling, as though ze'd been stripped of all hir juicy privacies by someone ze previously would have thought of as an ally. (These secrets were likely a precious resource that Emily had needed to haul before the tenure community at her university, Persia understood later.) Hir feeling of alienation was due, in part, to the academic phrasing strewn throughout Emily's piece. While Persia knew it would likely prove impossible to break the cycle of hetero-patriarchy without creating some new terminology, would it have hurt terribly much to throw a little poetry into the bargain? Didn't they all have a more lyrical way of talking about these issues, back in the dorm?

When thoughts of the old college crew cropped up, as they did tonight, Persia had to be on guard to avoid overestimating the possibility of like-minded communion in the future. It was good enough, in a way, to have experienced so satisfying a group dynamic once. So what if their contemporary Google Hangouts and gchats couldn't touch the fellowship of the old days?

Before long, the nostalgia muscles began to flex full-force, helping Persia reacquire a balance previously thrown off by hir pessimism. On this particular occasion, with Chilton Meyerbeer lightly snoring away in the shotgun seat, ze fondly recalled hir suite-mates' debates over Pop Art and the capitalism-wary Frankfurt School.

Heidi—who, at the time, edited a kicky feminist blog complete with a tube of lipstick in the header image—was a devotee of the Camille Paglia school, such that she considered the burning cross in Madonna's "Like a Prayer" video a foundational text of contemporary American seriousness. Winona, a Cherokee scholar-in-training on Weimar culture and philosophy, took the opposite view. Or, more precisely, she was prone to argumentation along the lines that whatever value pop culture may have had in dethroning stuffed-shirt theorists in the 1980s, such small-beer benefits had now been mostly processed and expelled by the organs responsible for regulating intellectual life in America. The lessons had been learned; the excesses of post-structural nonsense had been largely reined in outside of the Ivy League schools (which seemed unable to go on without such abstractions). What society was in danger of now was over-devotion to pop.

Last time Persia had checked in, Winona's doctoral thesis-in-progress was on the "ironic blind spot," what she otherwise called the "lacunae of intention," wherein appropriation of Kardashian-family paparazzi shots for one's withering blog (or Facebook wall) commentary was, often unbeknownst to the ironist, an activity that the various collaborative corporate entities behind *Keeping Up with the Kardashians* were counting on as part of their revenue stream. It was an argument she buttressed with the third volume of Marx's *Das Kapital*, which, even if it needed a little late-20th-century roadside assistance from Adorno's *Kultureindustrie* theories, could appear quite cogent in an academic setting. The entertainment industry, Winona recently concluded, had long since recognized and adapted to the use of pop's newly unquestioned superiority in culture consumption across all class markers and age demographics.

"But girl," Heidi might say, in the course of an email thread, exasperated by Winona's runaway train of rhetorical invective, "how can you confirm that the corporations know the route to profitability rests—even in part—with ironic pop-culture consumption? You've, like, seen the pie charts or something?"

At which point, Winona would lean into a familiar riff about the necessity of a culture-investigation tool similar to the Freedom of Information Act. "We need to see how companies are using market research to prey on our minds, our collective unconscious!"

Whenever Winona started to sound this wild, with propositions for cultural-landscape "game changers," Heidi knew she could count on the rest of the group's sympathies, which could be won on purely practical grounds. "Maybe that's true," Heidi would say, more than a little dismissively, "but since that's not ever going to happen in our lifetime, perhaps we should restrict our debates to the realm of the practicable."

In these moments, Winona was tempted to tell off Heidi to the effect that her people knew plenty about the realm of what was possible in terms of cultural revisionism—but by now, she knew it was not in her best strategic interest to retreat into the armor of Native American authority.

Persia missed IRL contact with these women, and others, too, from that undergraduate period of life. Not just the mood of fellow feeling, but the women in particular. Best ze knew, Heidi still maintained a blog of some repute. The last time ze had had a chance to read it, some years ago, Persia had been pleased to find that Heidi's writerly voice was now less inclined to adolescently sling a spaghetti strap off its shoulder to indicate the swinging, erotic-marketplace-value of its owner and proprietress. But Persia also knew that Heidi had married in recent months, the dick in question belonging to some grand family of Brooklyn Heights. Ze feared that Heidi's own intellectual projects might wither, if they had not already, when planted alongside the domestic chores that had become legion in that particular New York neighborhood.

Persia had lost track of Winona outside the Google Hangouts, ze was sad to admit now, as Chilton snored without interruption. The woman was hard to google, Persia had noticed at the irregular previous intervals during which ze had chosen to think of the old Wesleyan crew. But anonymity to search engines was not the same as having amounted to very little in the postcollegiate environment—Persia could hear Winona whispering a version of that sentiment into hir ear on this desolate Wyoming drive. Ze offered up, now, a private prayer to hir best memories of Winona, along the lines that she might be working with monk-like determination (and concomitant lack of public profile) on a campaign for prisoners' rights.

Persia even had occasion and expansiveness of heart now to wish the slightly silly and oblivious Emily well in her academic pursuits. So what if she had taken Percy's confidences a bit too lightly, and exploited them a bit much in that journal article? The woman very likely meant well, and was dealing as sensitively as she could—better than many other cisgender people, certainly—in her professional quest to understand trans realities.

It was during this extended moment, when Persia was in the process of having a beautiful thought for every one of hir old companions—forgiving each one for her faulty solipsism detector in such and such an instance—that Chilton elected to snort himself awake. *What asshole timing*, Persia thought, still annoyed with his general lack of forthcomingness during their day of travel.

He blinked in quick succession, as if it might bring the sun back up or beget something interesting to look at along the margins of the road. "We gonna stop at a proper place to sleep," he asked without any upward twist in pitch at the end of the sentence. It sounded like a phlegmy command.

Persia ignored him, and they rode in silence for another minute. While they had been driving—first from the airport to New Gaza, per Beverly's tip, and now further afield, to points of destination that, Persia had to admit, were not super clear—ze had thought about telling Chilton that ze was fairly sure ze'd actually seen Ghassan yesterday, running his stand-up act in a tent supervised by noted national-security threat Melly Shroud. Maybe that would keep Chilton awake. But then ze thought better of it.

"We're going to keep going along this highway. We'll head down every exit near a New Gaza camp and have a look-see around town." Persia patted the small plastic component outfitted with antennas that rested between them. "And we'll keep listening in on the scanner for police activity."

"In summary: you have no leads." Chilton didn't sound frustrated. In fact, he seemed more cheered at this juncture than at any other point in their travels.

"A key to good investigative work is knowing when to draw a breath," Persia said.

And it was at this moment Chilton first became aware that Persia was, in fact, still working. Chilton was a focus of Persia's investigation too—and since they hadn't located his half brother just yet, engaging him in conversation would certainly do, as a secondary objective. He reminded himself to be wary.

CHAPTER FOURTEEN:

CAMP ECHO WARDEN'S CHAMBERS,
GAZA, WYOMING
THURSDAY, AUGUST 6, 2015, 10:05 P.M. (MOUNTAIN TIME)

Normally, Clamp would have responded to the warden's email within 10 minutes. And yet an hour had passed with no response. Meanwhile, Homeland Security was leaving Lovegren voice-mail messages while he was on the other line talking to one of his contacts at the NSA. The contact was full of news about a black-ops CIA officer who was reportedly trailing another female journalist on the trail of the Meyerbeer case. That pair was due to land in Wyoming within the hour. *How many people knew about them?*, Lovegren wondered.

And about this silence from Clamp: was this the first evidence of mutiny? The warden had long ago predicted that the ambitious deputy would someday make a move against him, but had kept that prediction to himself; it wouldn't have helped to pump out any more mistrust than already flowed naturally in his offices. And in any case, he hadn't figured the betrayal to occur this week, this month, or even this year. Lovegren did not, as a matter of habit, enjoy trying to estimate the total amount of useful information he still had yet to pass on to the next generation of bureaucrat—it always led to self-doubt, as well as a sense of inevitable, encroaching obsolescence—but whatever the precise amount, surely his value could still be measured in positive, non-zero-integer territory.

Perhaps Clamp had indeed made a move. Hadn't even waited a full 24 hours, Lovegren guessed, before ratting out the warden's deal with the journalist and the damned Palestinian kid. If Philomela (bless her heart for being mistrustful) hadn't ditched the car as quickly as she had—at that godforsaken Tire Chief in western Wyoming, where Homeland Security had found the abandoned Lexus earlier that evening—Lovegren might have already been packing his bags for D.C., receiving a grilling ahead of formal termination of responsibilities.

As it stood now, when the tactical Homeland Security team had descended on the Tire Chief, all they had found was an empty New Gaza vehicle, tracking device intact. Lovegren could only hope that Clamp had led them there, with the guarantee that they'd find Philomela and Ghassan. The warden chuckled to himself. Absent locating Philomela or her foundling, there was no way for anyone to confirm the deputy's wild story about a Lovegren-sanctioned secret abduction.

Lovegren strode over to Clamp's office. The desktop computer was still on the desk—he couldn't have very easily run off with that under his arm, could he!—but otherwise, the room was strikingly bare of hard-copy materials.

The desolation bore the signal trace of youth in a hurry, and Lovegren, who was childless, surprised himself by being very near the precipice of tears. He had seldom shared a camaraderie with his deputy, let alone fatherly encouragement, but still, the betrayal stung. And Lovegren did not look forward to their next meeting, in which the warden would have to deny his entire role in the Shroud-Khouri affair. He would have to go full denial. So what if it was true that Warden Lovegren had written an email with the

164

subject line "Jailbreak"? Well, it had come from Lovegren's account, plain enough to see, but he certainly would never sanction any project so grave without taking more care to cover his tracks, no? (Please, Homeland Security middle manager in charge of contractor compliance, do give the senior bureaucrat some credit.) It stood to reason that the ambitious young deputy must have gained access to Lovegren's email account and fired off the supposedly incriminating note as part of his own machinations, now quite gone awry. In fact—yes, rifling through some emails previous to the aforementioned—anyone could see that it was the deputy who had first placed Ms. Shroud in proximity to young Mr. Khouri, right after she arrived in New Gaza. One was terribly sorry to admit that one had not seen the plot against the camp just a bit earlier.

Such a performance would buy him a day or two at most. But it would be enough for Lovegren to begin making countermoves. He resolved that his first would be to reconnect with the Democratic operative who had first disturbed his sleep, just two nights prior.

Yes, it was that man's turn to be bothered. The warden rang his number.

"Mr. Steindler, this is an appropriate hour, I presume?" It was already Friday on the East Coast—just after midnight. Lovegren laughed at his casually petty retribution.

"Warden—please accept, again, my apologies for the late hour when we first spoke." A brief pause. "It was thoughtless of me to assume that any high-level camp administrator would simply be used to late hours."

Lovegren smiled to himself. This neat-but-obvious form of cutting the warden down was Steindler's attempt at foreplay. "Never mind that," he said. "Can I take it that news of my fuckup is all the rage in Washington whisper-corridors, and that you're apprised of the semi-public details?"

Lovegren could hear Beverly take a deep, considered breath on the other end. "I suppose, first of all, I should congratulate you on being able to place this call," Beverly replied. "Unless I am your first call from some sort of detention center, which I would venture as being unlikely."

Looking around his own dim apartment—he had not left it still—Beverly Steindler wondered whether he was not residing in some highly bearable form of detention himself, perhaps the willing sort that belongs to bureaucrats too successful to find themselves undone or dethroned.

"Well, if I were, I doubt the detention center would even allow that legally cosmetic phone call," Lovegren said. "Tell me, what else do you know of my travails?"

"What makes you think I know more than anyone else in D.C.?"

The warden paused for effect. "Well, in point of fact, you knew about my troubles before I did." Silence on the other end. "Come now, isn't it so? Your initial call—you knew about the child, and the journalist."

Steindler's throat sounded dry. "Listen. I'm truly sorry about holding back," the operative began, after locating his voice. "If I'd known the budding events were so close to full flower, I'd have told you more. Please believe that."

"Right now, what extra knowledge do you possess?"

Beverly sighed. "I suppose I know that your troubles with journalists are not over."

So the warden's NSA contact had been right about that. "Which journalist?"

"My daughter, sadly, is one among their profession. Your name was already out and about in the near-open, so I gave it to her."

They were locked in a match to see who could appear more knowing. "Say, you wouldn't happen to know if she's coming this way with a CIA tail, would you?" the warden asked.

Beverly almost cackled with delight. It was as much fun as he'd had in weeks, going back and forth like this. "As a matter of fact, yes she does!"

"Don't sound so surprised that I have intel of my own."

"And she knows that he's CIA, as well."

"It's hard to keep a secret, these days."

"Oh, it really is."

CHAPTER FIFTEEN:

HERTZ RENT-A-CAR STAND,
CASPER–NATRONA COUNTY INTERNATIONAL AIRPORT,
WYOMING
THURSDAY, AUGUST 6, 2015, 11:00 P.M. (MOUNTAIN TIME)

"And if you could stop being so servile, that would be even better."

All through the flight, Eric had been attentive well past the point of politeness. He had hung on every word as his companion and ticket-procuring sponsor ran a monologue marathon—lecturing on everything from the cynicism of her bosses to the specific opportunity posed by the scoop they were chasing and what a rare opportunity the latter presented in terms of lancing, for once, the hideous boil represented by her employers. If she nailed this story, maybe she could swing to a proper network. Get out from under the web triumphalism of NewsPowMeow, which was really just profiting from the same old forms of audience underestimation developed by the "creatives" at ad agencies and venture capital firms.

It was almost as if he were performing a parody of internship, now that the jig was up. And she had obliged by being peevish and entitled, lashing out at the man who had duped and played her. With each of Eric's polite follow-up questions, Crissy's answers had grown more and more indelicate. In good-citizen mode, he had responded by taking on the silent burden of ensuring the comfort and security of those within earshot. In the terminal at Reagan National, he had craned his neck to see if a child might hear Crissy's next unsparing assessment of a colleague or filthy put-down of a friend-slash-competitor. He'd apologized to any scandalized mothers with pursed lips and rainbow-arched eyebrows. He had done his best to keep Crissy quiet, modulating his own voice down to nearly a whisper—even as his posture broadcast to all that he was doing everything he could to keep Crissy respectable in public. And yet her volume had only increased in the confines of the single-aisled jet that flew them to Wyoming. Now that they were in the rent-a-car line, she had decided that she had had enough, and would break him of the habit of apologizing on her behalf.

"I wasn't aware I was being servile."

"And isn't that often the way..."

The officious, ill-advisedly mustachioed Hertz official standing not two feet from their joint profile was unwittingly helping Crissy toward her goal. This hand-holder of consumer-facing tasks had offered only the slightest recognition—at the edge of the lips and in the almost imperceptible contraction of both sets of eyelids—that he had heard Crissy's insulting command to Eric. As though there were nothing odd at all in the air, he began his standard patter.

"And here is our Diamond Preferred Protection plan. If you read it, you'll see..."

After a brief moment of pretending to care, Crissy turned back to Eric, who was putting on a show of paying attention to the rental-car agent: part of his plan, she assumed, to make as many people as possible feel comfortable at any one time. The stare from Crissy would place a second, contradictory demand on his people-pleasing lobe, she hoped. But to her surprise, Eric was able to juggle this additional task; he began by giving her sarcastic little nods of the head as the comically unnecessary insurance upsell went on.

"Total security. Total peace of mind. If disaster should strike, the last thing you want to worry about..."

Impressive as Eric's wordless concessions to her cynicism were, Crissy was not in the mood to be silently tended to. With the Hertz man still exhausting the haranguing script he'd been forced to memorize, Crissy began talking directly to Eric as though they were alone.

"Men always play the decorous card through the first two dozen fucks or so." The Hertz agent slammed the breaks on his riff, mid–catastrophic-philosophical main clause. "Then the arrogant guns come out. I figure we've got another dozen or so nights together before you've got me weak enough to stomp all over me with your opinions. Why not just start now? Let me get a preview of what's in store, if this thing runs beyond a single-digit-night stand?"

"It would appear we're in something of a heedless mood," Eric told the Hertz man. "We'll take the cheapest level of insurance and be on our way."

Signing the rental agreement with one hand, Crissy held out the other—expecting the keys to a slightly dated but well polished Toyota Camry. She received them.

The exact location of Warden Lovegren's offices was not precisely findable on the rental vehicle's GPS device, though by the time they'd landed, Crissy knew that the drama had moved away from Camp Echo. Having reached out to Lovegren's office in the aftermath of her suspension, she'd made fast friends with a most helpful underling named Mr. Clamp. While she was on the flight with Eric, Mr. Clamp had apparently been willing to make mischief—emailing Crissy the address of the garage where the New Gaza Lexus had been found by Homeland Security investigators.

In the Hertz car, Crissy set to work punching in the address of the strip mall that was close to the garage. Just before she began to back out of the parking lot, Eric—seated shotgun—unbuckled her seat belt.

"It's cute enough watching you go all spy mode with your GPS, but how about you let me drive?"

"So I tell you to take control, and you just do it?" Crissy said after they had switched seats. Eric was easing them onto a highway that would have them near "the action," wherever that was, in a couple hours. "What a bore."

It was just before 1 a.m. when they arrived at a nondescript hilltop overlooking the Tire Chief garage and the strip mall. Spying her supposed intern checking the mag on a Glock and then calibrating his night-vision goggles, Crissy began to feel fear. That was normal, that was to be expected—but still, she didn't like it. She tried to dilute the feeling by noting how sexy her companion appeared, all official-security tough, as they stretched flat on the ground and looked at the dumpy garage.

The good Lord had seen fit to decorate the not-all-that-imposing hill with only the sparsest covering of vegetation, and Crissy felt the uneven hardness of the ground grinding against her ribs. They were approximately a hundred yards from the garage, where, so far as she could tell, nothing was afoot.

"So exactly what agency do you draw a paycheck from?" she asked to pass the time.

Eric brought a shushing index finger to her lips, holding the goggles with his other hand.

"CIA? NSA? Private government contractor who takes a side interest in Palestinian issues?"

He grunted slightly, not in anything like unambiguous confirmation. More like some barely polite recognition of her right to be filled in. "Something like that."

"Forgive a girl for wanting to know where the loyalties lie before shit starts jumping off."

"Don't use 'jumping off.' Sounds like you're trying too hard to be street," Eric said through lips screwed tight, goggles trained on a distant point of focus.

"Don't use 'trying too hard to be street,'" Crissy said. Eric's shushing finger came back.

At the same moment, from behind them came a sound that both Crissy and Eric—despite their vastly unequal training in weaponry—could identify as the unison locking and loading of several large guns. Eric lowered his night-vision goggles and modeled for Crissy the correct speed and posture for setting one's head on the ground while bringing one's palms overhead. A slight chorus of satisfied guffaws emanated from the dark periphery of Crissy's vision.

"I thought you were supposed to be good at, like, surveillance," she said, as she followed Eric's lead.

173

"Never underestimate home-field advantage."

"Now he tells me."

CHAPTER SIXTEEN:

VALUE-4-U COUNTRY SUITES,
UNINCORPORATED COUNTY, WYOMING
FRIDAY, AUGUST 7, 2015, 12:30 A.M. (MOUNTAIN TIME)

Ghassan lay flat on his nickel-thin mattress, both exhausted and awake. He assumed that Melly—who was not asleep either, the boy could tell—thought he was still in mourning for the abandoned country club's accoutrements. And while Ghassan had known civil war–destroyed West Beirut blocks that seemed less grim than the dilapidated darkness of their Wyoming motel, he was confident that low standards of decor were not the cause of his weariness. He did not miss his brief proximate relationship to the finer things. Instead, he felt sapped in the way one always did some hours after a well-intentioned Westerner had interrogated one's unwritten memoirs for information about how the world really worked.

Melly believed she could at least sketch the contours of Ghassan's biography by now. Being the sole offspring of a single-mom professor of comp lit at the American University of Beirut carried more than a few privileges—hardly limited to the fact that Mayssam Khouri had been one of the few Palestinians with permission to work legally in the country. Ghassan's extended family was a mix of Christian, Shia and Druze partisans, and the young man had apparently enjoyed the run of several properties in each confession's Lebanese stronghold—at least through middle school. That had all ended by 2014, though: a year when Ghassan lost not only his mother, but favorable immigration status, too. With Syrian strife spilling over into Lebanon, an uncle's invitation to bed down in the comparatively peaceful West Bank city of Nablus was viewed as the best move—though one the family came to regret in the aftermath of the Americans' projection of authority, later in that year. (As it happened, orphans did not fare all that well when Uncle Sam started determining who would be allowed to stay in the shrunken, noncontiguous West Bank homeland and who would leave for the American camps.)

Feeling exposed by the amount he'd told Melly in their relatively short time together, it now occurred to Ghassan that she had failed to listen to his oral history all the way up to the point where their paths had crossed in New Gaza. She hadn't shown much interest in his recent life in America at all. Typical mystical-orientalist American fixations, he thought.

"You watched my set, the other night," he said aloud to the pitch-black room.

"What?"

"At the camp. You said, when we busted out, that you'd first had the premonitory shock of possible recognition while staffing the amateur tent. You said you listened to my warm-up, and that you were there, that night."

"What about it?"

Ghassan laughed. "After all I've told you about my life, you can't tell me how the jokes sounded, out a piece from the stage?"

"'A piece' from the stage? What are you, a cowboy?"

"Everybody's a cowboy now," Ghassan said. "Even the Russians, and the Syrians too. The 20th century made sure of it."

"Whoa, OK there, *philosophe.*"

"If I convey to you the fact that there is an active Region 1 DVD bootleg market in Lebanon for titles never approved for sale in-country—and that even a few Hezbollah party-line voters may know of President Reagan's *Bedtime for Bonzo*—will that blow your mind so totally that you can't answer my question?"

"A lot of your jokes were good—until you rode them over rhetorical cliffs, like the one you just jumped from there," Melly said. Half-risen, now, from her unsleep, she was pinning her elbows into the slim comfort of the mattress, and letting her head fall back between her shoulders, as if stretching in the dark. "Why stand-up comedy, anyway?"

"The ex-reporter's curiosity is rekindled."

"I mean, it's possibly the very last American cultural tradition that I'd expect to translate into a Levantine teenager's fascination."

"*Levantine.* Fancy. Why not just say Palestinian?"

"Not sure you identify that way, first of all, after living most of your life in Beirut." Melly paused. "Do you?"

"Intellectually, as a political thing, sure," Ghassan said. "But not emotionally. I don't know; it's a lot of checkpoints, in my memory. Borders as an idea kind of fall away."

"So it's not wrong for me to say that you came to stand-up comedy as an idea in Lebanon."

"No, I guess not."

"Anyway, it still strikes me as strange. Your wanting to be a comic."

"Why?"

"Most of the other American cultural-performative pastimes are glamorous: everything from sports to competitive singing shows is based on a premise of putting a best, most aspirational foot forward. Which is why people in Ain al-Hilweh watch *Lebanon Idol*, too."

Ghassan laughed. "Look out, Miss Amreekah's dropping camp names now."

"Tell me I'm wrong," Melly said, in a voice of convivial challenge.

"No, I don't guess you are."

"But stand-up comedy works differently. The clown stands up and puts himself down before the audience can. I'm so fat, I'm no good at women, the sex I have is so terrible."

"Or there's the angry-screed school."

"Right, and that's where you come in. But that kind of comic is still an outsider."

Ghassan scratched his ear. "Your point?"

"You have to feel stable enough to volunteer for being an outsider, I guess."

"You're saying I'm privileged, then. That's an...interesting take."

Melly sighed. "No. Or, I don't know. It's definitely odd, though. Working at the craft of stand-up comedy in New Gaza. No other kids were doing it."

"A thing my mom used to say to her brother's theater partners in Nablus was that we became idealists over politics and pragmatists about culture, and made the wrong choice in each case."

Melly considered the value judgments, and the obverse of each, quietly before speaking again. "I'm pretty sure I know what an idealist politico is. But what did she mean by 'pragmatists about culture'?"

Ghassan didn't respond right away, and Melly reminded herself that this wasn't just an intellectual exercise for the kid; he was remembering a mother who had died in the Syrian civil war—not so long ago. "What did she mean? Hell if I know," Ghassan said. "Just a thing I've been told." Melly doubted that this was an honest response. But it would have felt unseemly to press for details.

"You know, that was bullshit just now," Ghassan said. "Yeah, sure: I know what she meant by that. She meant that politics is the art of the possible. You've heard the refrain about my people, I'm sure? 'Never miss an opportunity to miss an opportunity'? Even if, as with most absolutes, that slogan paints the issue with a fucking heavy hand, it's not wholly wrong, either. Before and after the Second Intifada—the time when, I'm told, we realized we couldn't take, nor would we be offered, steps to get any kind of real national determination from traditional political processes—we saw an uptick in shrugging acceptance in the cultural sphere.

"My mother saw enough women's health classes in the camps broken up by ambitious religious authorities, or by politicians who were uncomfortable with any citizen's increased knowledge of the female anatomy. Plenty of typically good people looked the other way when it came to repugnant Holocaust-denial rhetoric being trumpeted in speeches from certain quadrants. And my uncle's 'liberal' theater got shut down on enough occasions that each time he was allowed to reopen, the citizens knew to frequent it in steadily more pathetic numbers. So that's what my mother meant about becoming 'pragmatists about culture': while we held out for heavenly deliverance from worldly political problems, we looked at our own cultural production and, instead of mounting a resistance on that front, said, 'Eh, what can you do?'"

"Ah, I see," Melly said, though she wasn't sure she did. Mostly, she was hoping to sound sympathetic. "I mean: that makes sense. And don't feel bad about not answering my question, before. You don't have to tell me anything you don't want to."

Ghassan flipped on the cheap lamp between their slender beds. "So that was your own brand of bullshit, before? That I had to tell you as much as possible about my life, so that you could help us stay safe out here?"

"Turn the light back off," Melly said. "I was right about that much."

But they soon realized it was too late for lamplight strategy. After Ghassan followed Melly's instructions and they were pitched back into darkness, there came the thunder of what sounded like a convoy of pickup trucks, fast approaching. The sound of shooting rose into the air above their low-slung motel.

CHAPTER SEVENTEEN:

A WYOMING HIGHWAY
FRIDAY, AUGUST 7, 2015, 12:50 A.M. (MOUNTAIN TIME)

It wasn't as though Persia was fiending for juicy Meyerbeer family gossip. Ze simply wanted some chatter in the car, to keep things lively. Was that so wrong?

If Chilton was going to take hir up on hir invitation to drive them all over Wyoming—something Persia had offered as a deal-sweetener before he had elected to leave West Hollywood and hit the road, ostensibly to help out—ze decided the least he could do was talk to hir about more than the weather that stretched before them into dry infinity.

"So you really won't tell me any more about your work?" ze said. "It seems precious not to speak about the activity that takes up the majority of your conscious hours."

Chilton had a sneaky, gas-leak form of laughter: a hiss that came from nowhere, before bursting into some eruption. Despite the shock of his guffaw, Persia kept hir hands at ten and two on the wheel of the rental Prius that was powering them down the highway in a northeasterly direction.

"Sorry," he said after the chuckling had sputtered out. "I didn't mean to sound so dismissive." It was possible he was not terribly used to being challenged, Persia thought. Or used to conversation at all.

"Was it so hilarious a question to have asked?"

"Well," Chilton began—obviously enjoying the scansion of the line after having sounded it out to himself—"in the entire history of conversation openers, 'Please tell me more about your unfinished opera cycle' has seldom been adored."

"So perhaps you ought not to scorn this rare opportunity, then," Persia said with a cool tone.

Chilton paused, as if weighing the merits of hir comeback. "That's fair," he said after a moment. "But for now I still can't talk to you about my work."

Persia grimaced. "Because of this personal code—or is it a religion?—of would-be egoless silence."

"It's not all so set down or complicated as that," Chilton said. "I just don't like to talk about my work. And I think more people should take the same approach to their interests."

"To shut up," Persia confirmed.

"Yup." He stared out at the road. "How far apart are the camps spaced out, here in the flat horizon?"

"A good 100 miles between major internment zones."

"Lest a mass coordinated jailbreak occur, by noncitizens all."

Persia was feeling a need to correct Chilton at every turn. He had unsettled hir, ze realized. "Probably also the goal involves putting several buffer communities of regular American towns in between each locality that's up in arms over its bad-luck proximity to a part of New Gaza."

Chilton stroked his chin, as though assessing the likelihood of hir notion. Persia decided to cut off any possible rejoinder.

"Hell," Persia added, "I don't know why I said 'probably.' I know damn well how that was part of the calculation, as regards

camp spacing. You can check it in the *Congressional Record*."
Chilton fell silent, apparently satisfied with Persia's
comprehensive clarity—and with no indication that he had
registered hir dyspeptic tone. Fully maddening, his lack of
socialization.

"Eventually, you will crack," Persia said after a minute of
mutual silence. "I can see it in your face and hear it in your voice.
Whatever it is that stands between you and the act of holding forth
regarding your oh-so-many ideas can hardly be a weatherproof
structure. The winds of our association are sure to collapse it at
the seams."

Chilton smiled at the directness of Persia's assault.

"Your father is in the first stages of a run for the U.S. Senate
on the Democratic ticket," Persia continued. "I show up on your
doorstep with the news that I am investigating his background in
advance of the party's decision regarding which candidate to
support in a primary race. But at first you sit, seemingly bored, in
your recording studio in your West Hollywood manor, where
disdain is the posture to be assumed whenever the petty
machinations of politics darken a doorstep."

Persia pressed the button that recalled some portion of the
driver-side window into the door. The evening air that rushed into
the car created a stable harmony with hir voice, and Persia
quickened the pace of hir words, as though encouraged and
energized by the tonal company. "And this attitude changes only
when I mention that I am in pursuit of some spectral, not-even-
confirmed relation of yours—a half brother who would have been
conceived in the grayed-out period of your father's industrious
biography, after the dot-com-era boom-and-bust cycle and before

the finalization of his divorce from your mother. Only then do the temples spasm near your eyes, betraying a curiosity otherwise absent from your apathetic manner—"

Interrupting Persia's barrage, Chilton attempted a comeback. "You know you won't get me to talk about what I don't want to talk about just by making your speech more florid and ornate, don't you?"

They passed an exit, confirming Chilton's suspicion that he was the current object of Persia's investigative pursuit. *The real attack is soon to come*, he thought. *Stay prepared.*

"Don't be so sure," Persia continued. "In direct-voter-contact canvass prep, we train interns, college students and recent graduates to do basically one thing and one thing only when knocking on an unfamiliar door."

"Smile?"

"Not necessarily. Smile if the person's smiling, of course. But we coach them to be on the lookout for someone who's not smiling, or someone who immediately appears bored. If you're encountering a target who exhibits a scale-tilting amount of ennui after having lumbered to the doorstep, we counsel that a canvasser should appear likewise 'over it' too. We teach activists to 'meet the energy' of the person on the other side."

"That sounds pretty hippie-dippy."

"You're talking to me right now, aren't you? Surely you know that you have a terribly affected conversational voice. I've been speaking your language back to you, is all. I'm an expert in imitating the styles of others."

Ze had the feeling, just then, that Chilton had needed to restrain himself from saying something derisive and transphobic.

For Chilton's part, he was aware that he'd been wound up. By this individual. However you described Persia. Chilton had thought he was beginning to get it after the short lecture Persia had given him in the car. Persia VanSlyke was...how did it go again?...a fluid, genderqueer member of the trans community. He thought he understood "gynephilic." Chilton did like what Persia had told him about escaping gender-binary pronouns: "Ze" instead of "she" or "he"; "hir" (pronounced like "here") instead of "his" or "her."

Other parts of Persia's identity remained imperviously anti-intuitive to Chilton. For now, though—and of much greater immediate consequence—it seemed ze was correct about their current rate of verbal interaction: undoubtedly more words-per-minute had passed between them since leaving the warden's chambers in Camp Echo than at any other point in their time together. Though, in turning over the recent conversation in his memory, the sole legitimate son of capitalist extraordinaire Dennett Meyerbeer consoled himself with the understanding that he had revealed little of substantive value. Certainly nothing he had intended to keep from the Democratic Party operative, despite the chatty mood ze had inspired over the past few minutes.

"Why did you call it a religion just now?" Chilton asked. "What, about my preference to keep my creative efforts and ego to myself, amounts to monotheism?"

"Who said anything about monotheism?" Persia replied.

"Well, if you meant Buddhism, I suppose I would be flattered. But I suspect you had something less liberally commendable in mind when you dropped the R-word on me."

Persia smiled. Ze had meant to insult Chilton on this score, and was glad that he'd been smarting. "Your musicians are bound by nondisclosure agreements," ze began. "That feels pretty much like a secret order. Real gnostic behavior. Certain rites preserved for the initiated and so forth. And the monkish, reclusive mood tips over into the realm of martyrdom, too. Tell me where I've got it wrong, if you like."

Chilton now wanted a way out of this conversation, and badly. But defending his behavior would require the ceding of specifics better kept private. That was, after all, the whole point of his dedicated disavowal of publicity—and his refusal to publicly document his works.

"Who knows?" he said, making an effort to look like he was concentrating out the passenger-side window. "Perhaps you'll convince me to revise my attitude. But you'd need to do quite a lot of work, I expect. How much time do you think we'll be spending together?" This was better, talking in the conditional. Each breath spent in this voice was a flight from the contemporary and specific. "Yes, to get me talking, you would have to completely change me. To such a point that I might become immediately unrecognizable to myself, and then certainly willing to talk about a silly thing like my unimportant cycle of operas."

He waved one hand at the expanse of Wyoming desert, suggesting that the aridness of the land was as ill-equipped to bear fruit as Persia's line of conversation was to draw him out. Instead, he would show hir an uncompromising, humorless acreage of dirt.

"You can't believe it's unimportant," Persia said. "'My cycle of operas' is a phrase that has ego built right into its grammar. No one undertakes such a project just to keep it private."

Chilton sighed. "The only truly 'important' thing I can do is keep quiet about my egotistical pursuits. I can't refuse my ego, or its creative drive—especially because, unlike most Americans, I have the means at my disposal to indulge my inelegant fancies. But I can keep from talking to anyone about the inconsequential artistic results. I can, in short, decide not to be a self-important ass about it all."

As Persia drove, Chilton wondered if that point had been made strongly enough to end the conversation. Probably there was no way to stop someone from propelling a discussion forward when you were trapped in a car together. He could always ditch the vehicle and run screaming off at an angle, on foot, into the anonymous Wyoming winds, but then where would that get him? Privately, Chilton cursed the asymmetric warfare that is debate. It only took one dedicated person to keep a conversation alive; the sparring partner was merely dragged along by the force of insults and insinuation.

And so he decided he'd better keep talking. "Before you say that I must want some reward for my silence, or that I put myself above others on account of my private good manners, remember that you came to find me. If I stay silent, it is not to put on a show for you or anyone else; there is no endgame of public recognition. To believe that my actions amount to 'setting an example' that anyone else could even perceive—let alone follow—would be the most egomaniacal thing I could do. I know that.

"So instead, I simply make no public move. And I don't put my art into the world. I can't keep myself from having an active mind—I'm required to spend my time doing something. But because of the good fortunes of my family, I am not required to go and argue for the indispensable nature of this activity as a means to seeing that I am sufficiently rewarded for it. And so I don't. I take advantage of what is beyond my control—my family's relative comfort—to simply not go about being one more person in the attention-drawing hustle along the American avenue. And think what you will of my choice, but I will not make a public show of my thoughts in the future, either, no matter how this family business shakes out. If I should find a long-lost half brother at the end of our trek, I will try to win him over to my way of thinking. I'll provide the means to enable a similar stance on his part. Nor is this a posture. Recognition doesn't enter into it. I will try to impress upon him the inherent value of it, and keep him safe from you and whatever you and your fellow Democrats intend to do with him."

Chilton gasped, and promptly shut up. He'd said too much —slipped out of the conditional, due to an anger that stemmed from having to talk at all.

Persia adopted an innocent face. "We don't have any plans for your brother."

"If I have a brother at all. It's never been confirmed to me."

"If you do—it probably means the end of your father's nascent candidacy."

"Because the Democratic base hates the Palestinians every bit as much as the Republican base does. Isn't that right?"

"More or less," Persia allowed.

"It's only the professional class of Republican who has to stand behind the president right now. It's amazing, the improvisational hubris of the project. Solving the Middle East's problems one wildly myopic administration at a time.... And of course, the next Democrat will run against the whole misbegotten error in 2016—without having to fix it afterward, because it can't be fixed." Chilton smiled, after a long run of scowling. "Whether you know it yet or not, your team has the next election in the bag, if only you can manage to nominate candidates for the Senate who don't have illegitimate half-Palestinian teenage boys knocking around New Gaza."

"Well, you've stumbled onto a cause for some calm," Persia said at last, glad for Chilton's need to take a breath. "If you should have a brother, we'll have no quarrel with you in terms of keeping it quiet. We're not eager to have it public either."

Chilton snorted. "But that will only work out if dear old Dad is sensible about the matter. Which I am supposing he is not." He turned his gaze from the road to stare at Persia with an intensity that surprised hir. "Tell me: how many self-financing, billionaire would-be candidates are sensible about their families? Imagine for a moment that you say, 'Look here, Dennett, there's no point in continuing to go after the nomination. We've found your boy. It's all sewn up. If we could find it out, anyone could. If you run, it will come out—and we can't very well have a father of an interned Palestinian child running for office when the entire national campaign is about booting out the Republicans over the whole business with the camps.'" Chilton started laughing. "And then what if he says, 'I'll just run all the same, with my own money'? Even without the party's nomination, he'll still be a national story as an independent with liberal leanings and a tabloid personal life. And now you can see why I would prefer it if people kept more to themselves. The idea of public life leads directly to such horridness."

"Not all men are monsters," Persia said.

"A pithy effort. Tell me, though: How much do you know about my father?"

Persia had been trying to calm hir companion down with hir vocal tones and inflections—soft articulations and almost somnolently even timbres—but it had not worked. He was clearly agitated. So now ze boosted the cheer quotient artificially, hoping it would surprise Chilton and move him into another mood.

"Oh, not much at all, I'm afraid!" Persia ventured a quick, sharp laugh ze hoped Chilton would understand had been directed at hirself. But he didn't seem to be looking at hir. Persia needed to take another approach; ze narrowed hir eyes and stared at the man as ze drove.

"But this is how you would have others act," ze said. "It's obvious. You can't pretend that your starkness of attitude is not, ultimately, meant for public perception. Short of never leaving home, you're setting an example. The nondisclosure agreements for your musicians: you know they'll talk about the contracts, if not your actual self-suppressed music. Your actions are as public as your father's. You're a political animal too. That's why we're driving together."

"And what if I just want to find—and perhaps rescue—a potential member of my extended family?"

"People—and particularly politicians—are capable of doing things for multiple reasons," Persia said without venom. "And whenever 'family' is included among a host of motives, count on the politician to list that one first."

Chilton knew Persia was correct. The longer they were partnered on this journey, the harder it would be to evade hir questioning. But would it be so awful to take hir into his confidence after all? Chilton appreciated a few of Persia's qualities —the cocky clarity most of all. He announced to himself that he was not attracted to hir, not even a little bit, though he could not deny that he liked Persia's mind.

"You don't think that I might have found a more influential mode for broadcasting—or preaching—my values? If that was what I were truly interested in doing?" he asked after a minute's silence.

"I think you might have wanted a claim to obscurity. A plausible cover story. Very much like the one you're running now."

"That's hardly fair," Chilton said. "You'll be the worst sort of academic Marxist if every argument boils down to the fact that I don't know what I'm doing and am laboring under false consciousness."

Persia half-laughed. "Oh—but there's nothing false about your consciousness," ze said. "I think you know just what you're doing. It's canny. And besides, you probably haven't the patience for the more powerful forms of broadcasting. Working in an elite field of media, instead of some aesthetic backwater, requires an ability to get along. Being a staff member at a corporation means you have to shut up sometimes when you think other people are being idiotic or obvious—"

"I sense you may be talking out of personal experience here. Is that how it is for you in Democratic politics?"

Persia ignored the jab, keeping hir eyes on the road. "—and you might not have that skill. Pitching a fit from the vantage of contemporary opera composition might be the best chance you have of making a name for yourself and making the world pay attention to your ideas."

"Just out of curiosity: how many transgender people are there in mainstream politics?"

Persia glared at him. Chilton felt the sting of hir look and made a mental note to be more sparing with provocation on this topic. "Is this not a fair ground of inquiry?"

"As far as it goes," Persia said, "you may be surprised to learn that we are not so rare—even if we still encounter the visage of cisnormative shock and revulsion around every other corner."

"Well, at least now we're onto a field of real importance. Will it seem brownnosey of me to say that I respect what you do?"

"Investigating your father?" Persia said quickly, still sore.

"Well, yes, I suppose there's that," Chilton replied with a smile. "But please take the broader compliment. Party politics: you're right when you suppose that I haven't the patience to work in the places where real power is generated and sold off."

"There it is again. 'Sold off.' You can't even compliment someone in my position without condescending."

"The rapidity with which you are correct about the worst aspect of each thing that I say is breathtaking," Chilton said. And the sadness he used in announcing this observation succeeded in putting Persia off hir harshest battle track.

They drove down the highway in silence for a time, until Persia said, "I apologize if I was unkind about the compliment you were trying to pay me. It's just that—I suspected you were trying to annoy me as a strategy of getting us off the subject of your life's work."

He admired the Democratic operative's adaptability—it was the jujitsu art of someone practiced at making correct observations. Simply being able to see a situation clearly put

Persia in a stronger position to launch a new attack; ze earned a certain credibility one pose at a time. He would have to be on guard not to agree to every second observation Persia forwarded. "Hmm, yes," he said. "I suppose you are right about my motives there."

"Of course I am."

"But then what was the percentage in letting me rile you so easily?"

"Political operatives aren't perfect machines."

"At least not yet," Chilton added with a note of humor. "And thank God for that. It gives the rest of us a chance, still."

Persia smiled. "You don't invest much in chance," ze began. "If I were to hazard a guess, you don't think there's much hope for 'the rest of us,' as you put it in a very public-spirited manner. The only way someone goes full hermit, the way you have—"

"Hey!" Chilton tried to object.

"—is if he—and let us note that it is usually a *he* in these matters—has decided that resignation is the only defensible position."

"It's as though you've read some kind of terrible seduction manual for frat boys. You won't get me to open up to you just by flinging a battery of insults my way." Chilton had the feeling that he ought to be enjoying his comeback more than he was. But he was sore. The fact was that Persia was getting to him. He didn't feel close to breaking his vow of silence regarding his artistic pursuits. But as they pushed toward a future in which they might locate his possible half brother, all that he had managed to do up until now—and all the thoughts he had managed to impress himself with—seemed less important than ever before.

CHAPTER EIGHTEEN:

TIRE CHIEF GARAGE,
UNINCORPORATED COUNTY, WYOMING
FRIDAY, AUGUST 7, 2015, 1:05 A.M. (MOUNTAIN TIME)

The inside of the garage was lit by a series of industrial halogen lights mounted on floor stands, filaments covered with perpendicular metal bars that reminded Crissy of the face mask on a football helmet. The metallic shelves and gear boards holding the mechanics' grease-streaked implements cast a network of stark shadows against the walls. The angle of the light made the shadows distort upward, like the ones Halloweeners produce on their faces with flashlights. It felt as though there were no windows—or maybe it was just a dark night, Crissy thought. The bars on the lights projected crosshatch beams of darkness that Crissy might well have found intimidating in any circumstance— though she was aware that in this particular case, her fear was riding the coattails of their capture. They had been stripped of their phones and other electronics, and tied to chairs. Oh God, she saw one of the windows now—covered in black plastic. Was that a mortally grim sign? Eric was silent—but not stoically so. It was hard to gauge, but he didn't look like a man who expected to be shot in the next quarter hour.

A group of stubble-faced white male adults milled about in a distant corner, huddled around the man she had heard them call Rorty. Some were in better shape than others, but all of them looked revolting to Crissy.

"Every second we don't die, our odds improve," Eric said, finally. Like her, he was tied, tightly, to the seat of a metal step-stool chair—ankles and wrists clasped behind his back, at the coccyx, thanks to some handcuff-strength plastic bands.

"Yeah, but by how much?" Crissy said, surprised to find that speaking at all made her want to cry.

Rorty had been looking at them both closely, even as he addressed his compatriots. Now he broke away from the pack, striding over to Crissy and Eric, slightly favoring his right leg. Three other men—Rorty's lieutenants, Crissy guessed—took up positions behind him, spreading out and following him silently as they covered the 15 feet, give or take, separating the captors from their guests. A half-dozen lower-level soldiers kept their positions at the distant corner of the garage.

As he came into focus, Crissy saw that Rorty was surprisingly handsome. Even stray suggestions of a life lived not wholly under the attention of doctors—such as a stretch of acne scarring in the hollow of his left cheek, or the brown-edged crack in a bottom incisor—contributed an exciting if low-rent edge to the otherwise mainstream glamour of his conventionally presentable bone structure. Just as Crissy was thinking that Rorty might have benefited (even more than the other men) from better-fitting jeans, he spoke. His sound was universal hillbilly: g's had been banished to internment camps of their own, so that vowels could better stretch toward comic, taffy-gooping lengths.

"He is correct, my dear," Rorty began, in a bass register that ricocheted off all four walls. "Yeah, he's a real blazin' smart Federal, ain't he?"

Crissy said nothing as Rorty peered at Eric, walking closer. Arriving in front of the shackled man, Rorty poked at Eric's striated right shoulder muscle, which had been exposed by a tear in his shirt. That had probably happened, Crissy thought, as Eric was dragged into and out of one of the Hummers.

"So tell me, Federal," Rorty continued, walking now behind Eric and Crissy. "Why should we let you both live?" Sounds of mirth issued from the men at the opposite end of the garage. Was this riff very familiar to them? Perhaps outsiders were captured, strung up, and toyed with on a weekly basis.

"Is it because we have an enduring affection"—here Rorty pantomimed the soft patting of a cat, as though he held it in the crook of his arm—"for the U-nited States gov'ment?"

A quick peal of laughter from Rorty's men served as the response to their leader's call.

"That quiet sound from y'all makes me think you know that answer ain't close to the truth. Not even nearly so." By now, Rorty had spun back around in front of Crissy and Eric. "So I'll dispense with the suspense"—here he smiled at his perhaps unplanned rhyme—"and tell you why it is that you're still sucking air in our house."

Crissy flinched. Perhaps this had all been a prelude to a sucker punch in the face.

"Shit," Rorty said to his men. "She thinks this is all just to hurt her. She prolly thinks we're the real simple types: come together to rape women and do bestial things, and grunt and scrape at the floors to mark each passing hour."

Crissy could have done with some laughter from the group here, to prove that her fears, as correctly outlined by Rorty, were absurd. But none came.

"Much as you're sweet enough, and maybe enough so's that any one-a us would cross a street to follow yer into a parking lot"—a pause to let the grimness of that remark sink in—"that's not why we all here tonight. You may not see it, with your eee-leet-ist East Coast Ivy League eyes, but we're here to help America. For the benefit of us, and for you." Murmurs of approval rose from his congregation as Rorty emerged on the straightaway path to his main point.

"Like your boyfriend here told you, we coulda kilt you the een-stant we laid eyes on you. Through rifle scope, or through tactics closer up. But we're not into doing white folks in. Doesn't mean we won't ever do it. But we take no special pride...." Boots clomped in ragged syncopation.

"Hell, we're not even of a mind to pay much attention to the beaners no more. Nor any other brown types that come by their entry to this nation out of a desire to make better lives for themselves. We look back with heavy hearts and sweet nostalgia on the days when them folks was our only concern, it is true. And we just a-wish we could return to such times." Rorty kicked at the floor now, like a child on a baseball diamond expressing regret over the wild hop of a ground ball. "But that's not the reality we are called by providence to endure. Today, we have a separate problem—and I think both of you visitors to our blessed meeting hall know to which scourge I do refer."

Rorty made as if to dust off the collar of his grease-streaked work shirt. "The Palestinian says he is imprisoned here, in our great country," he continued. "But is it true? And if so, where else might he go about living? Nearly seventy years have passed since the destruction of Palestine. Thirty years ago it was they who were the plague that set a bloody civil war upon the Leb-an-eeeese people. Everywhere they go, these folks bring discord along with them—our humble nation only being the last to take them in and get spat on for the effort.

"Expelled from the camps in Jordan, expelled from the camps in Lebanon. They were homeless. Though it is now to our great sorrow, some of our conservative leaders, shaken by the pro-eeem-igrant policies of the recent past, were prevailed upon to take in these Palestinians. To give them sanctuary in our 'less populated areas.' But just because this decision has not resulted in the flourishing of the Palestinian people does not mean that America is profiting from them!"

A shout of "No!" came from behind Rorty. He held up a not-too-stern hand to recognize the utterance—and also choke it off.

"For, as with the beaner interlopers of the late aughts, what we see now is that the benefits flowing to the Palestinian residents faaaaar outstrip those that honest, Christian, American men can claim, here in the year two thousand and fifteen. And now, once you bear that wisdom in your heart, you see what a thick fat lie it is when they complain that they are held captive by us!"

Crissy—not having vocalized one way or the other her thoughts on what the Palestinians said about their condition, or what it meant for menial-labor availability in rural Wyoming— wondered if Rorty had forgotten to whom he was speaking. As her attention wandered, she noticed that Eric had struck a pose she heretofore would have associated with a subordinate in a short-tempered Communist bureaucracy. His attention was just short of rapt, as if he were prepared to salute soullessly at any moment. Perhaps Eric had been trained in hostage endurance, and this was the correct move. Crissy was not sure she could emulate his stance, so she turned back to Rorty and tried to pay sincere attention.

"Nor do we know, for absolute certain, through what power they appear in our midst!" Rorty said. "Oh, we have the official tales, sure enough. We know that our wise, quote-unquote thinkers in Washington felt that this would solve the issues dearest to their hearts, many thousands of miles away from the heartland! But who knows what the real reasons are? Or were? Not me," Rorty looked around the room. "Do any among you?" No one stirred, least of all Eric.

Rorty looked now to Crissy, and spoke to her in a tone slightly different from the one he'd adopted for the room. It was less down-home white-skinned preacher man and more akin to an inflection Crissy associated with furious press-office functionaries lobbying for a story to be killed or substantially amended. "Madam, you may think you are a random captive here," Rorty sneered. "You may doubt that those outside the Beltway even have devices that can handle the elegance of your high-definition news signal. But rest assured, your notoriety precedes you. And in fact, it is that fame that commends you to us, now, as we hunt for one of the rodents plaguing our state. Put another way: if you came to Wyoming in search of a hot story, we're going to do our best to show you one."

Looking back in subsequent years, Crissy would try to identify the moment when Eric had known for certain that he would not survive his time in the Wyoming garage. She had heard the lethal promises springing from the badly chapped mouth of Rorty—the man who passed as a visionary in those depressed parts. But when he had gone on for the better part of an hour, drifting back toward his followers in order to give the extended version of his lecture about the need to cleanse the American West of the interloping Palestinian menace, she was not fully convinced that the evening would, finally, amount to much.

When Rorty promised to bring Crissy a story, she did not immediately comprehend that he rather meant to do this. The reporter thought that Rorty, like many an untutored American, had presumed that his unedited editorial was the news. *The real scoop that the Eastern elites need to hear, if only they'd pull their fingers out of their ears and let the Real America speak with one run-on-sentence voice*: We Don't Need Your Liberal-Bias News.

At several points, as Rorty spoke, Crissy threw quick check-in glances in Eric's direction. Like Crissy, he had been positioned in a prayerful, halfway-bent-forward posture—leaning toward the center of the garage, into the sound emanating from Rorty. Mostly, Crissy hoped to share a mutual smirk. But she never snagged his gaze. For the first hour of Rorty's lecture, Eric continued to look on with the attention of a citizen in an authoritarian state—one fully aware that the price of even seeming to look distracted might be public disembowelment. Perhaps this should have been Crissy's first hint that Rorty's endgame would amount to more than bluster, and that she should have stopped thinking of him as some attention-starved redneck. If her shady, methodical, black-ops-educated companion was treating this seriously, perhaps she ought to have, as well.

As Crissy listened, she found herself wanting to object at nearly every turn—and not just when she disagreed with Rorty on first principles. For all his interest in the ways that the Palestinians had supposedly inserted their hands into American pockets, he seemed totally unaware that, before the United Nations began its midcentury relief work in the refugee camps of various Mideast countries, it had been American donors and activists who had held the world's humanitarian response together with the administrative equivalent of baling wire and duct tape. *If you're going to distort the modern-day fact pattern, why not root around in the past for other data ripe for distortion?*, she wanted to ask in front of Rorty's horde of admirers. Which maybe now included Eric? He looked ready to salute Rorty, if only he could raise his hand.

But she knew not to speak up. Not for so little gain. And, with her next glance, Crissy confirmed that Eric had not gone all Stockholm syndrome on her. He was, however, suffering from some other distress: Crissy had to smother an impulse to scream out loud when she saw him gnawing (with caution but also determination) at the very slender layer of fat stretched over the large triangle of muscle covering his right shoulder.

In future explorations of her memory, Crissy decided that her shock, at this juncture, likely had to do with more than the sight of Eric's own blood leaking down his chin. She was not skittish about the body. And it was about more than the steely look in his eyes. Was it possible that his brow was completely free of the simmering sweat Crissy would have expected to accompany this particular task? "Cold-blooded" took on a whole new meaning.

No, Crissy's alarm in this moment was connected to a perception she couldn't quite explain. And even though she didn't understand immediately what Eric was up to, she was savvy enough to realize that things were legitimately grave for them both. Eric, after a period of total mood effacement, was *making a move*. And though Crissy didn't presume to have too much black-ops knowledge, tearing open one's skin with one's teeth seemed like the first stage of a high-stakes, low-odds plan. Their lives truly were in danger.

Eric's eyes met hers for an instant. He rolled them, slightly, and accompanied their movement with a raised right eyebrow that asked, "Do you have to stare quite so much?" Now that she was aware of the developments unfolding just a yard and a half away, Crissy's desire to keep her attention fixed on each and every adjustment of Eric's jaw was understandable. But clearly bad form, too.

Meanwhile, Rorty's lecture was on autopilot. His audience was hypnotized; Eric had chosen this moment to bite into his shoulder for good reason. But if one of Rorty's gawking associates happened to see what Eric was doing, the plan was as good as scotched. And if it was Crissy's staring face that served as the pointing arrow, then that too would be unfortunate. So she returned her gaze to her lap.

Half a minute later, she heard a gasp. She hoped it had not been loud enough to attract attention. In any case, it proved too loud for Crissy; she couldn't bear not to look at her partner in captivity. She surveyed Rorty's coterie to see if anyone was staring, then swiveled her head. She was greeted with the sight of Eric's tongue prodding at what looked like a dime-size cystic bulge, right underneath the surface of the skin that he had already removed with his teeth. The number of capillaries leaking blood had multiplied in the past half minute; he could have taken his place in a cheap horror film's menagerie of extras, save for his general composure. Crissy did not immediately recognize the small bulge in his shoulder as a foreign object, but when the idea presented itself, Eric's behavior began to make sense. It was important for him to extract whatever had been embedded there; with his hands tied behind his back, extraction by tooth and tongue was the only option.

As Eric guided the object through his body with one last squeeze of the jaw, Crissy was reminded of home-movie-style childbirth videos she had seen. Eric's tongue gently oriented the item, still grasped tight by a subcutaneous layer of fat, before the last self-administered bite squeezed it loose. This mastication was the proverbial final push, the one that allowed what looked like an oblong pill to become fully born, there in the Wyoming garage. It also required a more forceful exhalation than Eric would have preferred—that being a full-on shout, in tribute to his frayed flesh.

At some point during these seconds—Crissy did not know exactly when—Rorty's speech had stopped, and all his followers' heads had turned in their direction.

Crissy later guessed that Eric's plan had been to hold the cream-colored pill in his mouth before passing it to the floor, where he could then have executed the next action item on his unannounced to-do list. And yet, with Eric's face twisted into a Francis Bacon–like portrait of agony, the pill had simply shot into the air. Its arc was not long defiant of gravity, but was still akin to a yogic parabola (and, to Crissy's mind, the sharp, downward twist was full of aching consequence). The pill skidded between Eric's chair and her own.

Rorty had started to march through the ring of seated admirers, heading toward the rear of the garage. As he passed, a man or two from each successive, cylindrical ring stood up to join him.

Crissy expected Rorty to be gritting his teeth, like a movie villain who has just discovered some covert plot launched by the shackled heroes. But he was smiling as he marched. He even had the presence of mind to brush the shaggy, layered blond tips of his mane behind his back with a playful flick.

Since the villain wasn't sufficiently troubled by whatever it was her black-ops companion had initiated, Crissy began to wonder if this was the end. She scanned Rorty's body for a holster, and found none. But surely one of his trailing goons was packing. She swung her face back toward Eric for guidance. He seemed focused on drawing in a full breath, instead of the shallow pantings he had been feeding his lungs with since his self-cannibalization.

At last Eric was sweating, Crissy noticed, just as the advance shadow of Rorty's approach reached out to graze their step-stool legs.

"Smash it!" Eric said. He didn't quite have the wind to finish the second word—stuttering across what, under normal circumstances, was a short bridge between vowel and consonant—but Crissy knew the "it" was the cream-colored pill. As she raised her left foot, she saw Rorty, in her peripheral vision, begin to make a sliding dive for the same part of the slate-colored garage floor.

Mashing it underfoot felt like stepping on one of those small New York City cockroaches whose size turns out to be a masterful cover for the million bones and beating hearts inside its compact body. The pill had packed an amniotic-like juice, which squirted out easily. Still, Crissy figured it wouldn't hurt to apply some honest, twisting torque, courtesy of her leather boot's heel. This move massaged a robust crunch sound out of the flattened pill. Rorty's hands were now grasping at her boot, trying to remove it from the object. Neither he nor Crissy had any real idea of what had happened, exactly, and so both took their attitudinal cues from Eric's sighing exhalation. The spy was still grimacing from his self-inflicted wound, but even so: his face was starting to relax.

One of Rorty's goons pressed a gun to Crissy's head. She promptly let up her foot.

"Let's guess: a tracking device?" Rorty asked, picking over the splattered remnants of the pill that had only minutes ago been secreted away in Eric's shoulder.

"We scanned 'em both for devices," the goon with the gun protested. But Rorty had been speaking and looking at Eric.

"Passive transmitter," Eric replied, eyes closed—as though he hadn't even heard the goon's extraneous utterance. His head was slung over to the left, in order to relieve his right shoulder from any and all duties related to posture. "Needs 75 pounds of direct pressure to activate. Wasn't sure Crissy had it in her." Had his body been fully operational, this last bit of flirtation would surely have come accompanied with a wink in her direction.

As things were, the only reaction Crissy earned was a grunt from a pistol-packing goon and a reflexive shove of his gun's muzzle into her skull. The goon smiled at his boss, perhaps hoping for an approving expression in return; instead, Rorty shook his head. His face adopted the exaggerated features of disapproval that kindergarten teachers use when trying to make sure children understand that a random act of aggression has proved not only unnecessary, but also notionally unwelcome. Crissy thought it a bit much—but then, sure enough, her goon seemed legitimately puzzled to have not received a scratch behind the ear for his hostility. The distance between the gun's muzzle and her scalp grew from nonexistent to about three inches.

"We don't need to treat our guests badly," Rorty explained to the room. "All they've done is something we would have done ourselves, in time." He looked at Crissy. "We promised them a good story; the point never was to hide our actions or our motives." Rorty turned to face the majority of his flock. "If they've invited more guests, that's not contrary to our purposes."

The roiling hatred beneath the surface of Rorty's faux hospitality was laid bare in the moments that followed, as his goons scattered about the garage, unsheathing machine guns and loading and comparing bazookas. Their acts of armament resembled a Victorian costume drama in terms of pageantry, and also suggested that the group was anticipating an incursion by more than a few of what they excitedly referred to as "hostiles."

Crissy had no way of knowing if this was merely rank paranoia, mixed with the red-blooded American rite of self-actualization through the stroking of weaponry. Even at this point, Crissy would remember later, Eric did not look resigned to certain death. If Rorty had wanted either one—or both—of them dead, there wouldn't have been any need for this orgy of stockpile undressing. A revolver to the head of each would have sufficed. Crissy felt awkward for feeling hopeful amid the preparatory chest puffing going on around her, and yet continued to hope for a nonlethal finish to this saga anyway.

CHAPTER NINETEEN:

A WYOMING HIGHWAY
FRIDAY, AUGUST 7, 2015, 2:15 A.M. (MOUNTAIN TIME)

"So, freshman year: 1994 at good ol' Wesleyan," Chilton said after a stretch of silence on the road to the next New Gaza camp, or maybe a hotel. He wasn't in charge, after all. "Postmodern academic liberalism at its period of peak alienation from the Democratic Leadership Council mainstream. That must have been a scene."

"Yes, if anything, it delayed my progress," said Persia. "The intensity of the turf wars made me timid. Who gets to claim what. I decided to claim nothing."

"And there wasn't a part of you that didn't thrill to the idea of overpowering that scene? Of changing everyone else's perceptions with your idiosyncratic individuality?"

It had been an hour since they'd eaten—greasy hamburgers at a roadside stand that was open at 1 a.m. despite the lack of foot traffic. Persia had snuck in a quick phone call to Beverly's house while Chilton took a whiz behind the nearby dilapidated Tilt-a-Whirl. But hir boss hadn't answered, and ze had no new intel on Ghassan Khouri.

Five hours had passed since they'd left Warden Lovegren's office. Persia hadn't a clue where to sleep for the night, and hadn't decided whether it was possible, or even advisable, to press on to the next camp before morning came. Perhaps they could nap for a couple hours in a parking lot outside the security perimeter at the next camp, before business hours commenced. In the meantime, talk would keep hir awake at the wheel.

"Exactly the opposite—I felt judgey about my own caution," ze replied, finally, to Chilton's question. "It took time. Once I conquered my fear about being gender-nonconforming in the way I wanted to be, I realized I didn't give a fuck about whether I looked like a man or not, or whether I would be confusing anyone."

"So, how does it go...with..."

"The ladies?"

"Yeah."

"Same as it goes for you, I expect. I have to find the women who are into what I have to offer. And seriously, that simple, mental movement was one of the first fully enjoyable moments of genderqueer living, the decision that it was already done—would require no surgery, or hormones, or explaining and self-apologizing. Fuck you, this is who I am. Here's how I like to fuck. You don't like it, here's a signed photocopy of my middle finger. I made a stack of a hundred at FedEx Kinko's, every one as special and individualized as each member of the transphobic asshole community that does not care to listen. End of story. And at the same time: I don't want to tell anyone else one way or the other how it needs to be for them. Nor do I have time for anyone coming up to me and challenging my use of pronouns."

Persia could see that Chilton was taking a moment for himself, the better to process such unfamiliar data. Ze said, "Tell me this isn't fascinating. Pretty eye-opening for you, no?"

"Right. So how can I continue to wall off my own interior life from your questions, is your next point. What with you being so comparatively generous."

"See: I think you've got potential. Most people look at a rich kid living in a 21st-century Xanadu, worshipping some obscure aesthetic gods, all while tending to an undernourished social life, and they say: that kid probably can't imagine his way into the head of a squirrel, let alone another human—and yet you've divined my train of thought exactly right. Time to spill."

"Jesus, OK. No need to be a raging dick about it."

Persia turned to give Chilton a quick moment of squinting side-eye. That remark. A question about what kind of anatomy ze might possess? Persia decided ze could let it go.

"So?"

"So," Chilton said, legitimately stumped.

"This is where you start to fill in details, say a little something about yourself. It's OK, we can start out with the bullshit self-narrative and work backwards from there, to the truth."

"Should I take the fact that you're joshing me harder as evidence that you're feeling a rapport now? The talk got a hell of a lot less academic all of a sudden."

"Stop stalling."

Chilton laughed. "Fine: standard boring bullshit, I guess. But if you want it: there was a private elementary school in the city, loads of test prep to get me into an elite public high school. I had a tutor for three years: this severe, über-fit blade of a young woman who was a part-time model, fitness instructor and freelancer on the test-prep scene."

"How often you must have jerked off, after lessons."

"Something like that. But really she taught me how to game every system without feeling bad about it. She told me that admissions counselors wanted people with my test scores, but who didn't seem overly impressed with themselves—and that my personal essay would be the place for me to communicate self-doubt and humility. She assigned my personal statement like an essay: asked me to come up with a way to express ambiguity, packaging it as yet another virtue I possessed as a candidate for entry into top colleges."

"How did you do it?"

"I had been, for a while, taking clarinet lessons from the first-ever African-American principal clarinetist in the Metropolitan Opera orchestra. He really liked Verdi—which was good, because the Met plays a lot of Verdi."

"OK."

"I take it you're not an opera person."

"Not really."

"Well, that puts you, for all your other idiosyncrasies of experience, firmly in the main of American behavior, you might be interested to know."

Persia tossed off a short laugh, as if to underline that this was not hir particular genderqueer project in life. "Goody," ze added for emphasis.

"Anyway, the short of it is: I lied on my essay."

"You weren't studying with the clarinetist?"

"Sure I was."

"OK, but so how did you lie?"

"In my essay, the black first-clarinetist at the Met wasn't as much into Verdi as he was into Scott Joplin."

"That's a jazz guy. I know that."

"Right. Or, you know, ragtime. He wrote an opera, too: *Treemonisha*. The piano score was lost for decades, in deference to our nation's long-standing ignorance regarding 'classical' music written by African-American composers. At any rate, the piano score was discovered in the 1970s; various grand-opera editions were prepared and premiered. My preferred recording is a chamber-orchestra version from the early 2000s. And in my college essay, I put responsibility for my *Treemonisha* affection in the hands of my clarinet player."

"Because he was black?"

"It made for a better story. The black clarinetist at the Met, who never gets to play Joplin's forgotten opera—even after academics struggled to produce a restoration score. Toiling away in the pit, tending to the orchestral legacy of white European classicism."

"Yeah, that has soulful first-person essay written all over it."

"But in actual fact, he was happy to play *Rigoletto* every season. He never uttered Scott Joplin's name at lesson time. Not even a single offhand reference to jazz. No Jelly Roll, no Ellington. I waited for a name-drop for two years, and it never came."

"You were dying for him to bring it up."

"Yup."

"We could have written an article about this at Wesleyan."

"This is what I'm saying."

"Making it all up for your college entrance essay, what you thought the admissions board would want to hear," Persia said.

"It's the kind of lie that would get a writer promoted at a magazine, until the lie got found out."

"But Princeton never caught me. I'm not proud of it now. I was barely even proud of it then. My dad wasn't around to give me counsel on the advisability of the lie. Though the first thing I remember him telling me was that 'to lie is to fear another man.'"

"But of course he was lying to your mother, when he was working abroad in Lebanon," Persia said. "Or did his enjoinment against falsehood really only apply to other men?"

Persia was interested in this—and could sense that ze was getting closer and closer to the real story behind possible U.S. Senate candidate Dennett Meyerbeer—but their conversation was brought to a halt as hir phone rang with a call from Beverly. The ringtone ze had assigned to hir boss was a revving motorcycle. A private joke about his ambulatory disinclination (and one ze wouldn't ever have wanted him to discover).

As Persia reached for the phone and applied the perfect pounds-per-inch friction to swipe the call into connectivity, ze thought harder about Beverly's struggle with moving about in the wider world, and harshly judged hir own decision to make even a moment's sport of it. In the fragmentary second before the call was connected, Persia took a free fall into hir memory. Ze recalled how little umbrage Beverly had evinced when ze had come out as genderqueer—even though ze knew he had likely hired hir, in part, due to hir onetime outward presentation.

Beverly had met that public Persia on the Wesleyan campus in 1998 by accident, though he almost immediately converted the moment into a practical opportunity; the Democratic Party senior operative was attuned, in that decade, to the possibility of a

Hillary Clinton presidential run, and aware that the party might best lay the groundwork for future electoral coalitions by organizing itself around the wide gender gap in the party's favor, among women. And then Persia up and announced hir genderqueerness on Beverly after graduating.

Now, ze held the phone up to hir ear and waited for him to say something. Ze could hear his breathing. Slightly labored. Not a new development, this. What was different from his usual phone demeanor was his tentativeness; in politics, one becomes accustomed to dispensing bad news. One even gets used to living in adverse climates of fact: here ze recalled the fateful afternoon when Beverly had sat in on Wesleyan's Campus Liberals Coalition meeting. Straight away the undergraduates, split as they were between the Campus Democrats and the Greens, had commenced re-debating the merits of Ralph Nader's third-party candidacy in 1996: whether he was right to run and, even if he had not been, whether he should consider doing it again in 2000. Next, the group fought over whether the two-party system was constructed precisely to rule out the kinds of changes that the Campus Ds said they sought. (Among those changes was increased aid for college tuition, regarding which: what a pipe dream! Persia had known even then it would lead nowhere, and had said so to the Campus Democrats.)

Whenever ze looked back at this moment, Persia refreshed hir astonishment at Beverly's patience in enduring the CLC's deeply unfocused conclave. Beverly always said the purpose had been to discover which of the activists was worth listening to. Though as ze learned later, another reason for his visit was the fact that the CLC's faculty advisor was an old friend from the New Left of the late '60s. Beverly's presence had been a favor to that old friend—a former SDS cochair who had since moved on to theorizing in the academic world—with the idea being that Beverly might speak to the group about what professional politics actually entailed (beyond airless debate). In any case, just because he hadn't come with the intention of scouting didn't mean he couldn't adapt to events as they unfolded. Thus, not five minutes after the meeting's erratic close—a nauseatingly earnest and naive prayer for unity—Beverly was giving Persia his business card.

"You realize I was just articulating the reasons why another Nader run might be good for liberalism," Persia had said to Beverly.

"Yeah, but you weren't too demagogic about it," Beverly said. "And you know what? For the first time in this whole fucking family-food-fight mess, I kind of understood why someone your age would still be holding the ingredients you're holding."

Persia hadn't known whether the extended metaphor was a compliment of the backhanded variety. And because Beverly had realized that it could be taken in such a manner, he quickly appended a grace note that confirmed the sincerity of the foregoing judgment. "Right or wrong, persuasion is the fundamental art of political operation. You can do it. So now it's my job to turn you in the direction of the apparatus where your powers will do the most good." He had already turned to leave the shabby basement room where, the Student Activities Committee had decided, the liberal students could fight out these issues. Back then, Persia had thought this was his high-handed way of leaving the room; now, ze knew his premature lean toward the exit was simply a consequence of Beverly's social unease. "Call me," he had said, almost to the adjacent stairway, and was gone.

"It's looking like probably a violent end," Beverly said on the phone now, as Persia drove through the Wyoming night on a probably pointless chase to find Ghassan Khouri.

Chilton was still talking in the passenger seat. Had been talking. Uninterruptedly.

"This is something that operagoers unwittingly abet," he was saying, quite without prompt. "Nobody says, 'I like novels.' People say, 'I like crime novels.' Or 'I like literary fiction,' whatever *that* is now. But opera fans persist in advertising their aesthetic preferences via a genus classification, as opposed to the species. Heaven forbid anyone say, 'I like *baroque* opera,' or '*Mozartean* opera,' or '*post-minimalist operas that would be far more likely to appeal to a contemporary-art, urban audience of—*'"

Jesus, Persia thought, *men*. Instead of articulating the thought, though, ze merely made a "would you please fucking quit it" gesture—and not without some difficulty. Keeping hir left hand on the wheel, and cradling the phone between hir head and hir right shoulder, Persia sliced hir free hand across hir neck. It was this bit of acrobatic sign language that, finally, brought Chilton's speechifying to a close.

Returning to the hard-breathing Beverly, Persia wanted to ask for more details, but was sensitive to the presence of hir passenger. Ze opted for a vagueness that still communicated plenty: "Which one? Both?"

"Both," Beverly confirmed, loudly enough for Persia to wonder whether Chilton could hear both ends of the conversation

217

via hir cell phone's tinny speaker. Beverly was now slow-motion choking on what sounded like a rather nasty (and possibly sentient) mass of phlegm.

"How do you know?" Persia asked.

"For the same reason that I can now tell you where to go," Beverly began. "I have sources who say a CIA officer just took out his passive homing signal, relatively close to the New Gaza camp where you were earlier today. And then the man activated it." Ze didn't know what that meant, exactly. But it did indeed sound grim.

Persia turned to Chilton, who looked like he was still sulking from having been told to shut it. Ze could take care of that—make him feel important by giving him a task to perform. "Get out your phone, and bring up a map," ze commanded, before getting an address from Beverly that turned out to be not too terribly far away from their current location.

After Beverly hung up, Persia and Chilton rode in silence for a few solemn minutes, until Persia became tired of the heavy mood in the vehicle. Ze felt sorry for Chilton, remembering that this was a family matter. The specter of a potent relationship—one he'd probably written an opera about—hovered over the events. Even though the two half brothers had never met, that still counted for something. When Persia had asked Beverly who was in particular danger, Chilton might have understood, as long as he wasn't totally checked out, that his brother was being discussed.

"So you were saying," Persia began, with a jovial lilt meant to raise both of their spirits.

If Chilton thought hir strategy was obvious, he certainly wasn't fast in showing it. He stared dumbly at hir for a few seconds before asking, "What?"

He wasn't asking hir to repeat the question—but instead hoping ze would explain to him what motivation he might summon to pretend that all was OK, and that banter was plausible again. The implicit question was too depressing to answer; engaging it would merely obstruct Persia from hir goal in cheering them both up for the remainder of the drive. And so ze said, "My God, don't you remember? You had me on tenterhooks, what with beginning to deign to tell me something concrete about your reasons for not allowing your operas to be performed."

Chilton smiled weakly, but said nothing else.

CHAPTER TWENTY:

TIRE CHIEF GARAGE,
UNINCORPORATED COUNTY, WYOMING
FRIDAY, AUGUST 7, 2015, 3:15 A.M. (MOUNTAIN TIME)

From a distance of what Persia estimated to be half a football field, ze and Chilton watched a convoy of three pickups approach the Tire Chief. Unlike Crissy and Eric, they had not left their car to conduct their nighttime surveillance. Positioned in the parking lot of the dilapidated strip mall directly adjacent to the garage, the car was angled away from the Tire Chief's neon, highway-illuminating signage, and was pointed in the direction of what appeared to be an abandoned nail salon. Persia used binoculars, craning hir neck to look through the rearview mirror at the garage that matched the coordinates Beverly had given hir on the phone. Chilton's assignment was to look through the front windshield and notify hir of an approach from any point along the plane of shuttered strip-mall storefronts.

"What'll we do if someone comes and asks what we're doing here?" Chilton asked.

"We'll say you have an urgent hangnail."

"M'kay. Place is pretty closed, though."

"How about we just start making out," Persia deadpanned, squinting through the lenses. "You'll just have to pretend that I'm a woman. Not that it's all that hard for cis folks to do."

Chilton was going to tell hir to knock it off when the gunfire erupted from the convoy of pickups parked outside the Tire Chief.

He crunched down in his seat, and Persia could tell he was no longer keeping watch through the front windshield. "Those weren't shots at anybody," ze said.

After righting himself, Chilton squinted for a second, then tapped Persia's shoulder by way of asking for a turn with the specs. Ze silently declined, partly out of possessiveness, but also out of a growing fear. Ze hadn't quite figured out what to do with the growing likelihood that Chilton would be meeting his brother under less-than-ideal circumstances.

"That's him!" Chilton yelled while Persia was grasping for a way to talk about the specific kinds of trouble they were in. "That's gotta be him, right?"

Indeed, *shit*, it was, Persia thought—recognizing the young comic, as well as Melly Shroud, from a distance. Ze could see about half a dozen sloppily uniformed gentlemen—all of them armed—leading the two less-than-eager individuals into the building's side entrance, which looked to be a retractable set of double garage doors.

"I suppose the responsible thing to do here would be to say we don't know who that is, for sure," ze lied.

"Man, that is some good politico cover-your-ass dissembling," Chilton said. He made a move to unbuckle his seatbelt.

"And where in fuck do you think you're going?" Persia asked. Chilton looked at hir helplessly. "To review: neither one of us is armed. We make two against their several dozen. If we call in the state police now, they'll be here with a tactical team within the half hour, and we can see what's what. And also: Homeland already knows that something bad is going down here."

The citation of other actors in their midst was a mistake, Persia realized immediately. The very idea of it replenished Chilton's fight-or-flight lobe with unthinking adrenaline. Before ze could reach out a hand to physically grab at his clothes, he was out the passenger door. Ze had no choice but to follow him, closer and closer across the deserted strip-mall parking lot, to the exterior of the Tire Chief.

Inside the garage, Eric had been passed out for more than an hour when several loud machine-gun rattlings put an end to the rest. "Fire coming only from one shooter," he said to Crissy after listening for a few seconds. "One location. Sounds celebratory, rather than actual engagement."

"So that's good," she said, not believing herself, as a pair of Rorty's goons put down their own munitions to clap at the fireworks outside.

After the two motors controlling the garage's west-facing wall had begun whirring, Crissy quickly recognized the figure of Philomela Shroud. The sight of the jailed journalist gave Crissy a sick feeling. It was odd seeing the woman in civilian clothes—a cheap-looking power suit that would have looked out-of-date in the 1990s.

Not that Crissy personally found Shroud disgraceful. The sick feeling was, instead, connected to the message embedded in her fall from esteem. Her reversal of fortune had carried a cautionary tale for all women in the profession: on matters of national security, you could not count on being treated as a macho soldier for truth, in the way of dissident male journalists. There would be no book deals, no invitations to talk with the ageless Charlie Rose. You would simply be thrown in a hole.

Standing next to Shroud—similarly frozen, in light of the gunmen surrounding the pair on all sides—was quite obviously the Palestinian child that the New Gaza deputy had emailed her about today. Possibly the same kid that Ms. Testington-Marglaze had been pissed off about. Possibly the son of Dennett Meyerbeer.

"Welcome back!" Rorty boomed, shaking Philomela's limp hand. The boy at her side was offered no greeting at all, Crissy noticed with the perverse excitement that accompanies a panning-out hunch. For a moment, Crissy forgot her own precarious position and let a smirk grow across her face. There existed a Palestinian child whose parentage was potentially significant enough that a New Gaza warden had contrived to let one of the NSA's most-hated journalists break him out. The Democratic Party was somehow mixed up in the plan, given that the child's father might be running for office in the near future. Everyone involved in the giant ruse might have succeeded, too, had it not been for the bad luck of running smack dab into a phalanx of nativists out on the plains.

It was a form of bad luck rather like the one facing Crissy now, she realized, coming back down from her reporter's high. As two of Rorty's henchmen brought out new step-stool chairs, she wondered if her comparative value as a target of violence had decreased, given the new arrivals. The well-known ex-reporter and the Palestinian escapee were both rarer finds than Crissy—she was just a regular, scandal-chasing journalist.

When Rorty next approached the prisoners' corner of the garage, he was holding more handcuff bands, and also some black rags. His goons frog-marched Shroud and the Palestinian kid into the chairs that had been placed in a row in front of Crissy and Eric. Rorty himself placed one rag each into the mouths of the boy, Shroud, and Eric. Once Crissy realized that no rag was going to be placed in her own mouth, her mind was flooded with a fear that came too late to do anyone any good. She wanted to take back all her caste-style thinking. No prisoner was any more or less valuable than another, she was now newly resolved to swear.

She looked at Eric just as one of Rorty's goons shot him in the head from behind. The bullet passed through and struck Shroud somewhere in the lower neck, it seemed to Crissy. The goon let her suffer for just a few seconds before finishing her off with a second shot from the gun, which no one had bothered to silence. The boy seated in front of Crissy could be heard weeping. Or was he a young man? The pitch of his moaning was too deep to be that of a boy. Nor did he even seem to have a conflicted urge to look at the slumped, expired body next to him. It occurred to Crissy that the young man might have seen plenty of dead bodies already.

"I'm going in there," Chilton said, crouching with Persia along a stretch of the garage's brick exterior. Yet he did not. Persia did not know whether to argue with him. There was no point, ze knew, in saying that the gunshots they'd just heard were perhaps celebratory, like the machine-gun fire they'd witnessed minutes ago. Ze was also aware that Chilton's bit of bravery might have been of the empty variety. Persia had already called 911—but whatever was happening inside the garage was going to happen before reinforcements arrived. And nothing ze and Chilton were

225

capable of doing would change that. Ze thought about noting, for Chilton's benefit, that one of the few things that could be worse than never meeting one's brother would be first setting eyes on him as he was murdered. Finally, though, ze said nothing, and Chilton made no move.

Looking at the back of the boy's head, and feeling for all the world like her mouth was as gagged as his, Crissy had lost track of the firearm. But when Rorty came around, she could see that the shiny, small black handgun had been transferred from goon to leader. As Rorty circled in front and raised his weapon at the young man, Crissy experienced a quiet previously unknown to her: the yawning silence that spreads across a room just before a bloodlusty group huzzah. She also realized, for the first time, that the next bullet might strike her, after it tore through the boy— whose head was still angled at the floor, refusing to meet Rorty's gaze or his weapon.

Crissy screamed: "No!"

Though the word had finally been ripped from her body by the realization that she was in the path of the next shot, it had not been fashioned purely in self-interest. She had meant "no" comprehensively. Crissy hoped that Rorty knew this. Still, he gave her a wink as he moved a step and a half to one side. He almost bowed as he did it, with a lordly courtesy. Looking back in later years, Crissy understood that there had never been a chance that Rorty would intentionally harm her. She remained unscathed for the same reason that she had not been gagged—because Rorty wanted a living witness. A reporter who wasn't in jail to see the crime.

Once the young man had been shot, with a single bullet that passed wide to Crissy's right, a lusty chorus of subliterate bravos occupied the interior of the Tire Chief. Leaning her head forward as far as she could manage, and with her arms still tied behind her back, Crissy vomited onto the garage floor.

CHAPTER TWENTY-ONE:

CHOPSTYX RESTAURANT,
POCATELLO, IDAHO
THURSDAY, AUGUST 13, 2015

It wasn't the best part of Persia's job, to be sure—though there was some entertainment value in watching a member of the leisure class try to "connect" with hir, while pressed by the twin exigencies of sociable humility and office-seeking. But sadly, the billionaire across the table from Persia this evening had proved duller than most. (Quite a feat, given the man's all-too-evident anxiousness.) Ze had spent the entire day with this cad, being shown about his hometown, forced to meet his old business colleagues. There had even been a supremely trying hour passed in the company of the ex–software titan's ex-wife. For this, ze'd been in a hurry to get to Idaho last week?

By the time of their one-on-one dinner, Persia's thoughts had turned to other matters. The death of Ghassan Khouri had scuttled the Meyerbeer campaign before it had even had a chance to kick into gear. The Romney administration had successfully spun the situation as the last bit of damage caused by Melly Shroud, the traitorous "reporter" (their air quotes). Warden Lovegren had been swiftly removed from his post.

For all Persia knew, Chilton was back in his mansion, resuming work on a masterpiece that he'd be keeping to himself. Crissy was already on the air again at NewsPowMeow. (Her suspension had been lifted as soon as her bosses learned that she'd placed herself at the center of such a hot story.) Beverly kept sending Persia new files. The 2016 Senate slate was looking progressively worse for the DSCC.

Meanwhile, the man at the table kept sucking back Lagavulin 16-year single malt on Persia's expense account. Chuck McClear. A would-be U.S. Senate candidate from the fine state of Idaho. Early-Retirement, Old Tech Money from the 2000s, and lots of it.

The Democratic Party's candidate bench in Idaho was not deep. And because the state's southeastern zone was fairly close to New Gaza, it was hard to know what kind of character to nominate in a Senate race. You had liberal pockets, committed to wresting the party back to its pre-Romney stance on immigration, but the farther one traveled east (and the closer toward New Gaza), the more the whole partisan switcheroo of the past few months—at least as regarded domestic immigration and the Middle East— appeared permanent. The Democrats had benefited, in the short term, from an influx of ex-Republicans disgusted that a Republican president had created a new class of immigrant. But then how long could the Democratic Party continue to depend on the fair-weather enthusiasm of nativists? Hard to figure, especially for state-wide races in the West.

It was possible that Old Tech Money might just pull off the neoliberal trick of seeming to appeal to everyone on the spectrum (before annoying everyone in practice). Thus he was getting his shot to impress Persia, who would in turn report to Beverly.

He'd failed to do anything but irritate hir. They had spent rather too much of the afternoon talking with his ex-wife, a severe piece of work who'd been coached by McClear—and maybe even a media trainer—to be as boring as possible. The obvious point of the exercise being that the ex-wife was ready to not be interesting, if the man who'd cheated on her and then paid a likely obscene amount of money in the divorce settlement were to became a candidate for the U.S. Senate.

Now they sat in an Asian fusion joint that looked like it had been stuffed inside an English pub without any thought for the clash between menu and decor.

"That Marnie. Wasn't she cool? And I don't mean 'hip,' but rather icily so," McClear asked Persia, finishing off the Lagavulin and signaling to the bartender for another without asking hir if that was OK, or even if ze'd like to refresh hir own vodka soda, which was almost at its end.

"Well, Chuck," Persia began, "you mind my asking what you ever saw in her?"

For the first time that day, McClear looked stricken by a question. He pulled at his tie, straining its Windsor. A bead of sweat started to form at his impressively forward-positioned hairline, which had, after 52 years, refused to budge even a centimeter away from the uppermost wrinkle of his forehead. "Well, this," he nearly yodeled at Persia, his voice breaking as if he were explaining slapdash homework to a skeptical teacher. "Exactly this: a campaign run. She'd have been perfect. She will be perfect, even in her diminished role as an erstwhile spouse. Believe it, no mistakes from her quadrant of my backstory. Will play her position true, not out of any undying loyalty to me, necessarily. If only from fear of embarrassing her own particular brand."

That was accurate, most probably. Even if this Marnie had first glanced at Persia the way you might look at an unfamiliar zoo animal. It might have seemed to the poor ex-wife as though Persia's square jaw didn't belong on the small body that it crowned. Likewise, hir prominent chin likely posed some unsolvable problem, when considered in relation to Persia's full lips.

This was an advantage Persia tended to notice, and treasure, when on the clock. As the individual opposite hir frittered away precious opening seconds trying (fruitlessly) to take in the measure of Persia's physical distinctness, the counter-opposition research specialist was learning all sorts of wonderful things. How freaked out the person could be over essentially irrelevant information, for starters. Or how smooth a potential candidate could manage to seem while in a state of confusion.

Chuck McClear was not cool, his billions notwithstanding. Persia was going to have to close this file tonight and tell Beverly the bad news: this was someone to develop as a donor to the party or a super PAC. But as a candidate, a definite no-go. Maybe ze could steer him toward seeing that his most useful role would be as a long-serving moneybags, scooping up checks from friends who had cashed out of AOL or whatever back when the cashing out was good. But this would require a sensitivity ze bristled at preparing hirself for; it wasn't the part of the game ze liked best, this snuffing out of dreams. Unless hir revelations were to be delivered to Beverly, the old campaign hand to whom ze owed hir career and hir comfortable life, Persia liked knowing more than telling.

"I'm going to take this call," Persia said, feeling the phone vibrate underneath hir leg, where it had been pinned to the chair, unobtrusive and out of sight but detectable in its thrumming.

"By all means," McClear replied.

"And then—just so you know where I've gone—I plan to use my exit from the table as a further opportunity to use the restroom, after hanging up."

"Little boys' or little girls'?" McClear said with no small amount of gloom.

This shit again. Did he know he'd tanked already? And if so, was this snotty comment his way of trying to know more about the person who was preparing to lower the boom—to tell him in no uncertain terms that he could stop right now with the wondering about whether the national committee would have his back in the primary—right after taking this call and then going off to piss?

"Well, whichever way I break, we'll have to agree not to describe it as *little* anything," Persia said to the would-be senator as ze rose from the table.

Make that the never-will-be senator, Persia thought, walking to the restroom hallway and answering the call from Beverly.

"So how did McClear look today?" he asked right off, without waiting for Persia to say hi or even indicate whether it was a good time for a chat.

"Bev, is it me, or have we not seen a legit candidate in months now?"

"It's not you. It's us."

Persia expected hir boss to move into peroration mode. They'd had this conversation hundreds of times before. Their joint

233

laments over saps like the guy Persia had seen today. Even if these rich pretenders to politics could be persuaded to give up the civic limelight, they would still want to "be a part of something." And in this way, men with money—the ones who couldn't pass a basic "do you care about the public?" sniff-test—might wind up with some ability to influence things.

Or else the party would be led by the scoundrels who were able to sell a barely plausible, hope-filled story of America but had terrible, almost inhumanly cruel scandals lodged in their pasts. Those knaves would eventually absorb the operative jobs like Persia's and Beverly's, after early retirements from new-tech this or global-synergy that. They'd run the Democratic Party "with some real business know-how," and fuck everything up worse than it had already been fucked up. And the Palestinians would languish in camps in the interior American West for at least as long as they'd been stashed in Jordan, Syria, Lebanon, Gaza and the West Bank.

But Beverly said nothing.

"Hey, boss," Persia said. "Have I caught you in a reverie? Shall I call back? If so, it's fine; I gotta take a leak and then try to convert this guy into a donor. 'The power behind the power,' that's the speech I'm getting ready to give."

Finally, Beverly spoke. "Are you near a television?"

"Nope. But if I duck my head back out into the dining area, I bet I can find whatever screen you're looking at."

"It's just that I think Christine looks quite good on the air tonight. Respectable."

Persia exhaled with moderate surprise. "Since when did you start watching NewsPowMeow, old man?"

"I expect it dates back to whenever I figured out that it was time to accept our world for what it is," Beverly said. "Couldn't tell you exactly."

About the Author:

Seth Colter Walls is a journalist whose criticism has appeared in *Slate*, the *Baffler*, and the *London Review of Books*, among other publications. He has worked for *Newsweek International* and Lebanon's *Daily Star*. He is grateful to Kate Bolick for her wise assistance at every stage of this book's development. Two editorial colleagues, Alex Balk and Choire Sicha, lent crucial early encouragement. Melanie Jackson's insights and agenting made the project feel more legitimate—as did Ana Benaroya's cover design and Silvija Ozols's copy-edits. Many thanks are also due to readers who provided valuable suggestions: Ruth Curry, Matthew Gallaway, and Brian Perkins.